AFTERMATH

Hurricane Book Two

BY JENNA-LYNNE DUNCAN
by JENNA-LYNNE DUNCAN

Stolen Kiss Press

Aftermath

Jenna-Lynne Duncan

Copyright © 2013 Jenna-Lynne Duncan

Edited by Rebecca Wahl
Cover art by Elaina Lee

Published by Stolen Kiss Press

ISBN-13: 978-0615882260 (Stolen Kiss Press)
ISBN-10: 0615882269

Library of Congress Control Number: 2013949771

To the inspiration behind all my romance writing,
who knows that even though my heart is in New Orleans,
it will forever belong to him.

.

Chapter One

❖

I awoke in the middle of the night to the feel of his warm lips pressed against mine. I pretended to be asleep for another few seconds before I was able to open my eyes to the night. "What's going on?" I became worried as I made out his profile sitting elegantly at the edge of my bed, fully dressed.

"I have to leave," Hayden said.

"Again?" I sat up, wiping away any mascara that may have been under my eyes.

"Yes. Again."

"No, stay." I tried to pull him down on the bed with me. That, of course, was physically impossible.

"I would love to." He smiled, lips closed, but the smile quickly fell. "You know I can't."

"Let Luke go. He can go by himself this time." I gave up my attempts to make him fall asleep with me, to make him forget that he had to leave.

"Luke isn't going."

"What?" I lay my head back down, feeling entirely too tired to keep my body up. "What are you talking about?"

"I'm going. Just me. Luke is staying here."

"No!" I stubbornly rolled my head into the pillow. "Remember what happened last time?" Last time being when he left me to go hunt a vampire and Luke stayed to 'watch' me. Instead, he had kissed me. His brother who I had thought hated me had instead confessed his love for me.

"I do." He placed a hand on my head and brushed a few strands out of the way. "The question is, why do you still remember?"

"Hayden…" I tried to sit up but was too tired to move. I took his hand in mine instead. Why was I so tired?

He leaned over and gave me one last kiss before I unwillingly let my eyes close for good that night. I knew he wouldn't be there when I woke up.

Chapter Two

✣

Our conversation rang through my mind as I woke up the next morning. I wished I hadn't said goodbye that way to Hayden. I wished I could take it back. This was one of the many times I wished I could go back in time and change things. I was so tired then, in a half-asleep state. I didn't even have the energy to sit up; my limbs felt paralyzed. *"Do you remember what happened last time?"* I mentally kicked myself for saying that. *How could I have said that? How awful Hayden must be feeling right now. Who knows what kind of dangers he is facing?* My only relief was in knowing that whatever he did, he was immortal. Still, what had bugged me the most was why *I* had said that in the first place. Should Hayden have to never leave my side just so I will never be tempted by Luke? Shouldn't he be able to trust me? Shouldn't I be able to trust myself? I was bent on making it up to him. There was enough anxiety in my life; I didn't need to add regret to my list. I pulled the covers off me and decided I would make this a good day.

I basically had the house to myself for the first time in a while. Hayden had left that night and Luke was never around long.

What *was* he doing all those nights? Honestly, it didn't matter. He was free to do whatever he wanted.

Since I was alone and had nowhere to be that day, I decided I should indulge in some girly pampering. I slept in late. I turned up the stereo and danced as I made the bed. I picked out a new nail polish color but decided to take a bath first. I ran the water in the tub but didn't have the patience to wait for it to fill. As I began to undress, I heard someone clear their throat, alerting their presence.

"Luke! What are you doing?" I ran to close the bathroom door on his face, but it wasn't his face I closed the door on. It was Hayden's. I reopened the door to make sure what I had seen was right.

"Huh?"

"Well good morning to you, too."

"You're back already?" I wrapped my arms tightly around him, thankful that I didn't have to wait to start apologizing for earlier.

"Back? I was just downstairs. But thanks for the enthusiasm."

"How did it go?" I considered not prying since he already acted like he'd never even left.

"Well, I was mistaken for Luke and I got a door slammed on my face. I've had better days," he spoke coolly, letting his dark hair fall into his green eyes.

"Did you not even leave yet?" Anxiousness shook my words as I thought about having to wait even longer for his return.

"Leave where?" A hint of worry in his confused eyes.

"Leave to… wait. Don't act like you don't know what I am talking about. You know you get all uncomfortable when I bring up Hunting."

"Ana…?"

"Last night you said you had to leave, and that Luke would be staying. C'mon!" I waited for him to confirm what I said was true.

He pulled his eyebrows together. "I'm sorry, Ana, that never happened."

Crap. He pulled me into his arms as the realization came over me that it was all just a dream.

"It was so real this time. I could smell you, and feel your kiss."

"I'm sorry. It's killing me that I haven't been able to figure out why you can see the future in your dreams. Since Katrina and the Lalaurie incident, they are cautious. No one is talking. If I wanted some definite answers I could go to a friend on the West Coast but you know I can't leave New Orleans right now."

"'S okay. Really, it's fine. I should be so lucky as to have dreams about you kissing me." I looked up at him to make part of my dream into reality. "They just are beginning to feel too real though. I mean, I didn't even know it was just a dream. So does that mean you are leaving?"

"I don't know, am I?"

"I hope not. Too bad I can only see the future and not change it. Why didn't I get a useful abnormality?"

"If I recall, it has proven useful, Ana. And who says you can't change the future?"

"I have never been able to before." I bit my lip remembering the horrible consequence of trying to tell my school's guidance counselor, Mr. White, about his wife's impending death. I didn't even want to think about the helplessness of having a psychic dream about Hurricane Katrina.

"Just because you haven't before doesn't mean you still can't."

"So you wouldn't mind me trying, then?"

"Trying to change the future?"

I nodded.

"If anyone can do it, it would be you." He wrapped one arm around me to pull me closer. "But…"

"But?"

"But…I think we should focus on what the Vasquez said. It could be very dangerous if word gets out about your…ability. Agreed?"

"Agreed." *For now.*

"Even though you didn't leave, I missed you."

"I can fix that." He grabbed me with both arms now, pulling me into a kiss.

"Do you want to answer that?" He pulled back at the sound of vibration coming from my night stand.

"No?" I tried to pull him towards me but he gave me an exasperated look. "Fine." I ran towards the bed and flopped on my stomach to grab my phone in time. The screen lit up with three letters I hadn't seen there in a while. *Dad.*

"Hi, Dad," I answered. I heard the water turn off in the bathroom and looked back to make sure Hayden hadn't yet left. It was my dad so I knew the conversation would be short.

Hey babe, what's going on?

"Nothing, just at home right now." I still couldn't get used to saying 'home' and meaning in this mansion, with Hayden. "Why, what's up?"

I have a break tomorrow; do you want to go out for an early dinner?

Hayden and I had plans after school. I looked back at Hayden, knowing he could hear, and mouthed *sorry*. He nodded.

"Sure, dad. I'm free." I winked at Hayden before turning back around.

K. Should we meet at the restaurant or do you want to me to pick you up?

"I'll just meet you there."

Hey Ana?

"Yeah?"

Where's the truck?

My heart stopped and every muscle on my body paralyzed. Hayden didn't need to hear what my dad had said to be able to see that all the blood had drained from my face.

"The truck?" I managed to get out.

He laughed. *Good thing you evacuated with it huh? To think, it might have gotten flood damage.*

"Ha, yeah, to think…" I was in *big* trouble. I had forgotten all about his truck. I was at the supermarket when I had been kidnapped and pulled into Hayden's car as it sped away. If it was still there and not stolen, it would have been under a couple feet of water from Katrina. Why did he want the truck anyway? He drove his girlfriend's car. "Why do you ask?" I tried to turn the tables.

Well I just thought about selling it. Since you're always driving with Hayden it's probably just sitting in the garage, ain't it?

"Sitting in the garage. Yep." I tried to laugh but it sounded like a groan.

I just thought you could drive it to the restaurant when we have dinner tomorrow and I could drive it back.

I turned back to Hayden to signal help with my eyes but he was already gone. "Maybe, dad. But I gotta go. Love ya, bye."

Um, love you…"

I hung up the phone before he could ask any more questions. What was I going to do? "Hayden?" I yelled as I ran into the hallway.

"Down here."

I flew down the steps to find him at the computer. "What are you doing? How could you leave me like that? I am totally dead!" I paced in front of him, knowing there was no possible way to get out of this one.

"No you're not." He didn't find my expression funny. "I am finding you a new one."

"Oh, I know! I could stage a carjacking!"

"You wouldn't lie, Ana."

"I kinda already did…"

"Besides, I am taking care of it."

I was too caught up in coming up with lame excuses to give my father that I didn't hear Luke come home.

"Seriously, what am I going to do?"

"What? Can't figure out which outfit to wear?" My head whipped toward Luke who was lying on the couch drinking a can of soda.

"I'm not in the mood Luke." I pinned him to the couch with my eyes.

"Whoa, sorry." He stood up and walked over to look at Hayden's computer. "What's going on?"

"Oh, Ana is just being overdramatic because her father wants his truck back."

"Overdramatic? How am I being overdramatic? It's not like he's asking for a book back, it's his truck. It's probably a $10,000 truck, for which I have no idea where to start looking. Even if I do find it, it probably won't even start!"

"Ana, don't worry. I said I am finding you a new one."

"What do you mean 'a new one?'"

"There are thousands of trucks for sale that look just like yours. We just have to find one with similar mileage that's mechanically sound - so one *not* in New Orleans."

"So, you're going to go and buy me a truck, just so I can give it to my dad so he can sell it?" I was incredulous.

"Yes?" He looked at me like it was a completely feasible option.

"That is a good chunk of change that I don't want you spending on me. I am already living with you. You have done enough for me."

"For the last time, you don't need to worry about the money. And I think it is only appropriate since it is our fault that your car is gone in the first place." His voice faded but he failed at distracting me.

"You're right! I would still have the truck if you hadn't kidnapped me!"

"You might not be alive if we hadn't kidnapped you so I guess we're even," Luke butted in.

"Fine." I felt a little better about the situation. And it could work, it could actually work.

"It looks exactly like it," Luke said to Hayden as they looked at the computer screen.

"It's in Texas."

"Yes, but it looks just like it. It has the same ram bars and everything"

"Oh, no." The blood drained from my face as I slumped into a chair by the computer.

"What's wrong?" Hayden beat Luke to asking.

"This means you're leaving doesn't it?" I remembered my dream all at once.

Hayden remembered too. I just wasn't sure what part of my dream made his eyebrows furrow in hurt. "No, I am sure Luke can go pick it up."

"I can?"

Hayden let out a tormented breath. He knew he would be wasting his time if he tried to convince Luke to go instead of going himself. I wondered if he knew that because he believed in my ability to predict the future, having already seen him leaving in my dream last night, or more appallingly because he knew this was the opportunity Luke had been waiting for. "I will go on the next hunt alone if you will do this for me."

"No way. I have school, *remember* brother?"

Hayden shook his head. I had almost forgotten that tomorrow was the first day I would be going back to Ecole Classique High School, the private academy I attended, since Hurricane Katrina. Hayden and Luke enrolled as students before Katrina hit and would continue to play the role as normal teenagers, but Luke was only trying to fool himself into pretending he cared about something as mortal as high school. Hayden couldn't even look in my eyes as he walked past me, heading toward his room upstairs. I gave Luke a death stare before running after Hayden.

"What'd I do?" Luke said behind me.

It was unusual seeing Hayden alone in his room. His room was clean and smelled of him with a hint of something else, something I couldn't figure out yet. I had never looked at his room this way before and I realized I was looking at it as an outsider and not something we shared. The thought burned the edges of my heart and I tried not to add guilt to that feeling by remembering what I had said to him in my dream. He came out of the closet, throwing a small black duffle bag on the bed. Something clanked inside that told me there was something other than clothes in it. I hadn't seen Hayden this upset since I'd had a death wish and had stolen his Porsche.

"I'm going with you."

He smirked, pulling up one side of his smile. "You can't." His head hung, and he didn't take his eyes off of a blade he examined. *Oh.* So definitely not clothes in the bag. How many weapons did he own?

"I am not staying here alone."

He sheathed the blade and put it in his bag. "You won't be alone." He looked at me now as if to gauge my expression. "Luke will be here."

"I don't want to be here without you." I walked over to him, stopping him by wrapping my arms around his neck. He looked away and I tried to catch him with my eyes. "There is no reason I can't come with you. It's not like it's anything dangerous." My thoughts flashed to his arsenal and I wondered if maybe he *was* going to be doing something dangerous.

"Tomorrow is your first day back at school since Katrina and you have dinner with your father. It would look a little suspicious if he asked about the truck and then all of a sudden you didn't show up."

I could have argued with him. It would have probably gone something like this: I demanding that I was going, he refusing, and then I ultimately begging to go with him. But what that said was that I wasn't capable of being alone, or that Hayden couldn't trust me alone with Luke. There was no uncertainty in my feelings for Hayden. There was no reason I couldn't be alone, even if it was with his brother, with whom I had shared a passionate kiss on the beach.

I pulled Hayden into my lips. He would be gone for a night and I had to stock up on the kisses I would lose. I licked my lips in invitation. His eyes changed and something sultrier took over him. He exhaled one breath, letting me know I had won at least one battle. I smiled as I returned his kiss. He always kissed me like it was his last.

I jolted awake to find myself enshrouded in darkness. Not even the muted sunlight lit up my curtains. Somewhere between watching Hayden pack and get ready, I had decided it was a good idea to lie down. I looked at the clock; it was 7:30 pm. I hated sleeping like that; I wouldn't be able to fall back asleep again until dawn. I looked around the room. No Hayden, just like I had dreamt. A pang of sadness shot through me along with déjà vu. At least I was able to succeed in assuring him of my intentions before he left. I picked up my phone. I had a few missed calls and texts but the only one I focused on was Hayden's.

> Hayden: **I left for Texas, but you already knew that. I love you, and even though you already know that too, I will never stop telling you.**

My heart ached even more than it had before.

I got up and decided to do something productive. I called Marie to tell her all about the dream I had during my nap. Another nightmarish dream that I hoped wasn't a prediction. Nikki and Marie had been very accepting after I told them everything, well, almost everything. Marie, surprisingly, believed what I had said right away. Nikki on the other hand was harder to convince. Luckily, my dreams were cooperating and I was able to predict a few things to Nikki. I scared her off for a good week but she came around. Pretty soon she was back to the same old Nikki, joking around and thinking my predictions were humorous. She asked for the lotto numbers on more than one occasion. Marie was oddly the supportive one. She was the first one I would call after a dream.

I described the attack I saw in my dream. "The scenery sounds a lot like Lafitte," she noted. She was right. The swamps and the walking paths in my dream did look like Jean Lafitte National Park. I hadn't been there in years so I had no idea what it could look like now. "But there are a lot of places in Louisiana that look like that, so…" she added after my pause.

"Yeah," I agreed, but my mind focused back to my dream. I wrapped things up with Marie, realizing that the house seemed too quiet. I wondered if Luke had left me alone. It was completely dark as I walked downstairs. I looked to the couch, where I expected to find Luke flipping through channels. A sole light shone from the kitchen. I walked apprehensively towards it, raising my bare feet unintentionally to my tiptoes.

"Luke? What are you doing?" My heartbeat leveled, feeling relief that I was not alone.

He looked up at me from the breakfast table. "Reading a book." He held it up with one hand as evidence.

"You're reading?"

"Yup."

"A book?"

"*Yes*…" He sat the book down now, looking me square in the face from across the table where I now sat. "Why is that so hard to believe?"

"It's not; I just didn't expect it is all. So, what are you reading?"

"Oh, just some book I found of yours."

I scoffed. Of course he went through my purse. "Well, do you like it?" He would say no at which point I could say that he shouldn't have been going through my stuff.

"Actually, yeah. It is really good. I haven't been able to put it down."

I raised one eye brow at him but he was serious. I let out a laugh before it disappeared. Looking out the door to the backyard made me think about the dark swamp I saw in my dream and the jogger who went in unknowingly.

"What's wrong?" Luke scooted his chair closer to where I sat; his scent pooled in the air around me. I held in a breath. Luke chuckled and adjusted his chair. Dang, I hated how he knew his effect on me. I couldn't hide anything from these two, especially not the quickening of my heartbeat as a result of my embarrassment. Thankfully he moved further back so I found it safe to breathe again. But I hated the fact that I should care about how good Luke smelled in the first place. His scent was stronger than Hayden's and completely different. Hayden smelled like summer and Luke, like autumn. He smelled sweet-yet-earthy, like oranges and dried leaves.

I shook my head. "It's nothing. I just had this dream…" I thought if I talked, it would keep my mind off other things.

"Tell me about it," he said before I could brush off the topic.

"I don't know anymore, Luke. Why am I dreaming of these things?" The question was rhetorical and his lips curled down and waited for me to say more.

"I had a dream last night about Hayden leaving and despite anything he or I tried to do, it still came true, he still left. What is the purpose of seeing the future if I can't do anything about it? I don't know if I will have an ordinary dream or a horrible dream when I close my eyes. I took a nap today and dreamed of an attack. It was someone I didn't know, in some place I didn't know, or maybe I do know but what's the point?"

"You know the place in your dream?"

"Marie had said it sounded like Lafitte and maybe she's right."

"Then let's go." Luke stood up grabbing his keys off the kitchen counter.

I followed. "Wait, what? What do you mean 'let's go'?" Adrenaline rushed through my body at the thought.

"You keep sitting here, beating yourself up about what you see. You want to help, you want to change the future but you're afraid to do anything about it."

"I...I'm not afraid. I just thought it was too dangerous. You know, the whole protecting me bit?"

He raised his eyebrows at me, answering all my questions at once.

"You really think I can change what I see in my dreams, to stop it from happening?" I became more and more excited at the thought of him believing in me, believing that I could do something about it.

"Well not *just* you. But you and me? Hell yeah." He smile was infectious and I couldn't help but returning the look. "C'mon." He grabbed my arm, sending a numbing sensation throughout my body as he pulled me toward the garage.

Inside Hayden's black sports car, I second-guessed myself. "What are we doing? I mean, really? Who knows when this is going to happen? It's only after nine, we could be waiting all night. "

"What are you afraid of?" His hazel eyes met mine and my chest immediately constricted. I held his gaze only briefly before the smell of autumn caught in my nose.

"Let's do this." I shifted in my seat and turned up the volume knob on the stereo.

He smirked as he thrust the gear in drive.

What was I afraid of? That wasn't an easy one to answer. Sure, I could pretend that I wasn't afraid at all, and that is surely the face I would be giving Luke. But that was a lie. Was I afraid of whatever kind of animal it was that attacked the passerby? Was I afraid that I wouldn't be able to stop it? That I would be too late? Or maybe I was afraid of the feelings that were developing in me as a result of Luke's unconditional faith in my abilities.

It took thirty minutes to drive to the national park, and with the stereo loud, I spent the entire time chipping the polish off my nails and thinking, or rather, second-guessing. *What was I doing?* The closer we came to our destination, the more anxiety I had. I came up with a million different excuses to turn around and go back home but when we got to the entrance, I didn't need any.

"Oh, it's closed. Too bad. Well, at least we tried."

"You're kidding, right?" Luke pulled the car to the side and got out.

"What are you doing?"

"You don't think we came all this way to let a little gate stop us, do you?"

When he saw that I wasn't getting out of the car he came around and opened the door for me.

He bent down to face me. "What's wrong?"

I looked at my hands, trying to decide what to reply. "It's a swamp."

"And?"

"And I'm afraid of alligators, okay Luke?" Maybe it was the fear of going into a swamp at night with hungry alligators that had been ticked off since the hurricane or maybe it was something more. Either way I didn't want to find out.

"You've been hunted by a ghost and driven eight hours with a gang of Hunters who wanted to kill you and you're afraid of *alligators*?"

He was right. I hated when he was right. I was not the same person I once was. I had become stronger, I had to be stronger.

"C'mon. Not to wound your pride or anything, but, more likely than not, I am going to be the one that is protecting us here. I *am* immortal; an alligator is the least of my worries."

I nodded once and got willfully out of the car. It took Luke only a second to open the gate. His nonchalance about it gave me just a glimpse into his world.

"You said you dreamt of a jogger?" Luke asked as he stepped through the gate.

I followed close behind. "Yep."

"That's weird."

"What's weird?"

"It's weird that someone would go jogging in a state park after hours, especially one that you claim is filled with alligators."

"Hm. I guess I never really thought about that. I never said this was the exact place, I couldn't be sure. It's just what I saw, okay?"

"Okay, Okay, I believe you."

The lights on the car went off automatically. I jumped forward, almost knocking into Luke. My heart sped up and I could hear the blood rushing in my ears. Luke laughed.

"Will you stop listening to my heartbeat?" I barked at him.

"I can't help it; it's so loud I could hear it from Terrytown."

"Ha-ha," I mocked. My eyes were adjusting to the complete darkness but the moonlight was not enough for me to see where I walked.

"You have no idea what it does to me knowing how close you are to me right now, but could you stop stepping on my heels?"

"I am a human remember? I can't see anything in the dark."

"Oh yeah, woops." I heard the rattling of a key chain and then a small flashlight turned on.

I grabbed it from him. "Thank you." I shone it on the scenery around us, hoping something would spark a memory of familiarity. We walked about ten minutes in and the smell of swamp hit me. It was probably all around us.

"Anything look familiar yet?"

"No, for the last time." I was ready to give up, until I saw a bench. It was just a small resting place for walkers but it looked like one in my dream. "Maybe this bench? I don't know, I can't be sure."

"OK, well at least that's a start." He sat down.

"What are you doing?"

"Waiting.

I shone the light in his face, looking at him incredulously. This was not the Luke I knew. "You really have that much faith in me to sit here and wait who-knows-how-long for who-knows-what?"

"Don't you get that already, Ana? Yes. I do."

I shrugged and sat down next to him. Gooseflesh covered my arms; it was the cool air of a New Orleans winter. I had barely managed to grab shoes in the excitement as I left the house. I looked at Luke; he looked perfectly comfortable in a black t-shirt.

Impossible. I tried to rub my arms to produce heat by friction. My cold hands only chilled me further.

"You're cold?" He asked surprised.

"Uh, yeah? It's like 40 degrees out here!"

A unique expression came over his face; it was of confusion, then pain. "Oh, I'm sorry. I didn't realize..."

"Aren't *you* cold?" I shone the flashlight over his t-shirt for effect.

"No, Ana. I don't get cold. Or hot."

"Oh. I hadn't thought about that." He still held the same expression, thinking. I continued, "I guess there is a lot I don't know about Hunters." There was hint of sadness to my comment, which I tried to hide from him.

He suddenly stood up, taking off his t-shirt.

"What are you doing?" My back straightened as I choked out the words.

"Keeping you warm." I moved the flashlight abruptly off his torso. If he thought my heartbeat was loud before...

"Here, put this on." He handed me his shirt and I obeyed. It was still warm when I put it on and gave his autumn scent a stronger, more home-like feel.

"Thanks. Are you sure you won't be cold?"

He laughed. "No, Ana."

"Okay..." I wished he would have just kept the shirt on, which would have been less awkward than knowing he was shirtless beside me.

"So, what's the plan?"

"You're asking me the plan? I thought you'd have one."

"It's your dream, you know all the details."

The beauty of his facial features in the moonlight distracted me. "How'd you get that scar?"

I tried to reach out to his face and touch it with the tips of my fingers. He pulled his eyebrows together and turned away. "It's nothing."

He exhaled a jagged breath. "It's from the night my parents died." I pulled my hand away and placed it on top of his, not forcing him to say more about how his parents were killed, but hoping he would. He turned his hand, palm up, entwining his fingers in mine. A tingling sensation shot through my body.

"Something's coming…"

I jerked my hand away at his comment. "I don't hear anything."

"Shhh…"

I turned off my flashlight, my hands shaking in the process.

A minute later I heard quick footfalls on the leaf-covered pavement. Adrenaline rushed through my body; the shot of blood to my head caused it to spin. My heart pounded against my rib cage; anxiety and joy took over as I realized I was about to witness my dream coming true first-hand.

A few things happened simultaneously. The man approached us, Luke stiffened, and I turned the light on and jumped up to stop him.

"What is this?" The jogger skidded to a stop. His postured erected like he was ready to defend himself.

Luke got up with me, standing to my left. His eyes were scanning the darkness around the jogger. Upon seeing a shirtless and muscular Luke, the jogger started to run in the other direction.

"Wait!" I yelled after him. Luke held out an arm to stop me. I shined the light on him, his chin rose and his gaze narrowed in the opposite direction of the jogger.

"We're not alone." He let out what sounded like growl. Luke pulled me closer with his arms. "You ready?"

A tried to force a swallow and nodded.

"Whatever it is, we've disrupted its plan, and it's not happy about it. The jogger is no longer its target. Listen to me, Ana. You need to go back to the car immediately. I'll take care of whatever *it* is. Go now." Luke disappeared beside me and I didn't hesitate to think about how I was alone in the dark swamp. My legs took off under me, faster than ever before. The adrenaline pushed me harder and faster.

'*Whatever* it *is*?' That can't be good. That definitely can't be good. My heart raced but my breathing remained steady. Should I be worried about Luke? No, surely he could handle whatever was out there. I stopped running and looked in both directions, not sure which path to take. I had to listen to him this time, to stay out of trouble and meet him at his car. But the energy that flowed through my veins told me otherwise. I felt like I could take on whatever was out there. But I didn't want what happened last time at Club Skye to happen again. There would be no Hayden or his parents to bail me out again. I looked down at myself, realizing I still wore Luke's shirt and it saddened me. He was here because of me. Because he believed in me, and if anything happened to him because of it...

I looked one final time in the direction Luke went and started running toward him. I ran for a few minutes, feeling like the darkness was about to close in on me. Fear prevented me from stopping, a high kept me going. Luke's black t-shirt clung to the sweat forming on my body and I finally slowed to a fast walk.

"Luke?" I whispered knowing I didn't need— or want -- to yell in order for him to hear me. Seconds passed with nothing but the sound of locusts and bullfrogs. But then even those quieted and there was pure silence around me. I had whispered his name again before I heard footsteps behind me. My heart froze in my chest. *Luke.*

"There you are! I've been trying to find you, are you all right?" I turned around to look at him, but there was no one there. I shone my flashlight in every direction. Still, there was nothing. Nothing but dead silence. And then the sound of footsteps. I turned in each direction, always hearing footsteps behind me. Maybe I just didn't know where they were coming from.

"Luke, it's not funny." If he tried to scare me, I swear—

The sound of the footsteps got closer. My ears were ringing and skin burning from a painful chill. An instinct inside me warned me and I took off in a run. "Luke!" I yelled, tearing my vocal chords as I started running. Yes, I definitely had to run. I ran faster than before, still hearing the footsteps trailing me. They were catching up to me, and getting louder and louder as they hit the ground, sounding like a horse trot on hard pavement. I gasped as something stung my back in one sharp movement causing me to fall to the ground, face first. I turned on my back ready to face whatever was after me. I felt the ground around me with my hands, hoping by some stroke of luck that the flashlight had just turned off but had not broken. A bead of warm liquid slid slowly down my face. It felt too thick to be sweat. Blood. I sat up feeling the gash on my forehead and cringed at the pain. My breathing heaved as I waited for whatever was in front of me. It was as if it enjoyed tormenting me this way. I tried to make out the dark shadows around me. Nothing was there until all-at-once something dark and heavy was on top of me. I kicked it off me with such force I heard its friction against the ground. I thought about running again, but I knew it would just keep coming after me. I had to kill it, but how? Was it man, animal or something other entirely?

I stood up preparing to find something I could use as a weapon. The shadow rose taller than me and then the shadows multiplied. Like the thing had split in two because there were now two things on either side of me, surrounding me. In what felt like hours passing, not seconds, I flashed back to Halloween night at Club Skye. I pictured the Hybrid, a disturbing combination of a pig's head and a man's body. The pig-head craned its neck to the side, its black, empty eyes boring into mine. The corners of its repulsive mouth drew up into what appeared to be a smile. A satanic smile. My whole body shuddered. Luke was there. He'd pushed me forcibly behind him, his body tensed and positioned in a crouch. His broad shoulders had blocked my view of the hideous creature. He had been protecting me that night but I had no one to protect me now. Luke was prepared to fight then. *How could I let this happen? I was supposed to save his life but he ended up risking his to save mine. Something wrapped tightly around my neck, choking me as I was lifted into the air. My feet were set on top of the bar, but the tightening around my neck was not released. I felt the blood start to pool in my face. There was only one person pressing against me from behind, but too many arms imprisoning my body. One around my neck, each arm and leg, my waist... Luke turned around and looked up at me, determined. My vocal chords didn't work as I tried to call out his name...*

I should fight the two dark shadows approaching me. I should never give up. After everything I'd been through, I couldn't let this be the way I died. I couldn't let them kill me so easily. But I was frozen. Frozen in the past. Locked in the memories of just one of the many times I would almost die.

A gush of wind, one after the other, blew past and the dark shadows were gone as far as I could see. A new presence came with the wind and I knew that the shadows hadn't just left, they had fled. This was getting fast out-of-control. The sounds of bugs and nighttime creatures returned and I knew I was alone for the time-being. "Luke!" I called out to him again, my voice shaky and sounding like a cry. Where was he? I knew he could hear me. Why did he have to believe in me so much? This was a stupid idea. I found myself wishing Hayden was there, for once appreciative of his over-protectiveness.

I felt the ground with my hands, working my way over to the trees. I dug through the cold mud, pulled up a promising branch to use if necessary, and started moving once again to find Luke. I debated whether to walk or run. Running didn't pan out too well last time but as I heard the impending silence around me again, I knew it was my only option. Before I could sprint, I felt a hard, angry arm around my waist and I was lifted into the air, upside down. I still had the stick in my hand and was prepared to use it until I realized what, or who, had caught me.

"Drop the twig, Ana"

"Hayden?" The combination of his touch and smell brought back all the familiarities at once.

He didn't answer. I let out a slight squeal as I was thrown over his shoulders. Hayden felt like a rock underneath me. "Hayden?" I pleaded for some sort of response, and when I didn't get one I changed my tone. "Put me down! We have to find Luke." *Wrong words.* Hayden tensed slightly at my comment.

I heard footsteps in front of me, and I quickly panicked.

The footsteps slowed "Whew!" *Luke.* "All I have to say was what the f—"

"Shut it, Luke."

"Geez, somebody came back from Texas cranky. Ana is that you?" I slumped against Hayden's death grip, my mind running through everything that happened in the last ten minutes. I had lost Luke, possibly come close to death, and Hayden had returned early from Texas. "Damn. I thought I told you to go back to the car!"

"And you expected her to comply? " Hayden scoffed sarcastically.

Hayden dipped down and picked up the key chain I had dropped earlier. The adrenaline that ran through my body now eased, leaving me a headache from the extra blood that shot through my head. I winced.

"Are you okay?" Hayden and Luke said simultaneously and I felt Hayden's head snap in the direction of Luke. There was too much tension in the air. I dreaded when I would have to answer questions about what I was thinking to go along with something like this. Even though it wasn't Luke's fault, Hayden would blame him anyway.

"I'm fine," I finally answered.

When we got to the gate I only saw one car and wondered how Hayden got here.

"Where's the truck?" I mumbled.

"Home." He clipped. Uh oh, the one word answers were not a good sign.

The lights on the car flashed as it was unlocked.

My head throbbed again as Hayden sat me down in the back seat.

"*I'm* driving," Hayden said as a command to Luke.

Luke threw up his arms in surrender. Not even *he* wanted to push Hayden any further tonight.

"Hayden..." I started, as we pulled away from Lafitte.

"Not now, Ana. I'm not ready to talk about this now." His jaw muscles clenched.

"Why the hell not?" Luke butted in, obviously deserting his previous position of not pushing Hayden. "You can't shelter her from the Underworld forever. She needs to know, has to know! She saved the guy's life for God's sake. This could be something."

My eyes shot up. I *had* been able to change the future?

"We are *not* doing this now," Hayden said through his teeth.

"Whatever, man. It was amazing. *She* was amazing. Think about it, now we don't have to go Hunting later. How lucky did we get that this thing, or these things, weren't human?"

Hayden froze at Luke's last word. But his emotions quickly changed into something else. Anger? Jealousy? I didn't know. "Are you really that stupid? You could have gotten her killed! I know you're all bent on destroying your own life but leave *my* girlfriend out of it. You say you love her but then you put her life in danger. *If* you truly loved her, you would leave her alone. She is with me. Whatever you are trying to do to prove otherwise is not working and is going to get her killed!"

"Don't even start with me. Yeah, yeah we all know your sob story. Well, who the hell cares you've been waiting a hundred years for her? She is my true One and you know I will never, *can never*, stop trying to make her love me!"

"Whoa, hello? I am right here. Stop fighting and stop talking about me like I am not right in front of you! I was, once again, almost *killed*. That may seem like a walk in the park for y'all but I am freaking out back here and have a killer headache so if you guys could, please save your displays of testosterone for another day." Hayden whipped around a curve before finally slowing down. I rubbed my temples, trying to make the throbbing go away.

"No problem, babe." Luke turned his head to wink at me. That was apparently the last straw for Hayden. The car jolted to a stop and I hit the back of Luke's seat. A new pain shot through my head.

"Ah, shoot!" I said with my hands over my face, feeling like I broke my nose.

"Ana, I'm sorry. I didn't mean—"

"Just please take me home," I moaned.

"*What* is your problem, Hayden?" Luke turned toward me, holding out his hand to touch me. I was too busy cringing in pain to notice what was about to happen. "Are you ok, Ana?"

"Don't. Touch. Her." I heard a thump and my eyes shot open. The drive felt like it took forever. *Please let's just make it home.*

I leaned through the middle, creating a barrier between them. "This is ridiculous. *You guys* are being ridiculous. Please just stop. You are brothers, or did you forget? And I really don't have the time, energy or desire to play referee, especially when it's about me." I dropped my head, gripping it with my arms. I felt the car start moving again and a few minutes later the fluorescent lights of the garage lit up the car. The engine went off and no one moved until I lifted my head.

Luke's hand was on the handle, his torso turned to exit. "Just so you know, this isn't about the curse or what has happened between Ana and me. This is about her. Just her. And I believe in her, something you fail to do. If you haven't noticed, Ana isn't one to sit back and not do something. She's not made of glass; she can handle herself. She can be something more and tonight has proven that. Just as she has believed in me, I will never stop believing in her." The car door slammed behind him.

Hayden helped me out of the car and we walked inside toward the kitchen. He handed me a bottle of water out of the fridge and two headache pills from the medicine cabinet.

"Thanks," I said before popping them in my mouth. I thought I would need the whole bottle with the way I felt.

Hayden looked me up and down for the first time, noticing my over-sized male shirt. I squeezed my eyes shut not wanting to explain, or not knowing how: either one, I just wasn't sure at this point. When I opened my eyes, sympathy displayed all over Hayden's face. I sighed, taking a step into his arms, my hands curling to his chest. He kissed my hair multiple times and I finally felt the pain subside.

Chapter Three

⚜

"That was awesome!" I came down to the breakfast table the next morning, my hair still damp from a shower.

Luke and Hayden shared the same look of curiosity and confusion. No one commented in return and I was too impatient to not continue. "Last night. That was—"

"Crazy? Dangerous? Stupid?" Hayden looked at Luke with the last one.

"—Incredible!" I sighed. "The running, the excitement." I slammed my hand down on the counter for effect. "We saved someone's life. Someone's *life*, can you believe it? I dreamt about it. We went there and it came true right before our eyes and then BAM- we stopped it. How amazing is that?" I sat down at the breakfast table next to Hayden. "I can't wait to do it again." I molded into the chair with a sigh.

"You sure did a one-eighty from last night," Luke spoke.

"Feeling better, I suppose?" Hayden smiled at me and leaned in for a kiss.

"Yes. I feel great."

"That's amazing considering you had a bad headache last night, it's just after six *and* we have to go to school."

"I know. It's weird, isn't it? I just feel like I have so much energy. I just want to run around or something. I can't wait to do it again."

"Do it again?" Hayden eyed me, trying to hide his nervousness.

"Well, I'm not exactly sure how this psychic thing works, but yes, I would want to, *have to*, do it again."

"How about we just get through today? It is the first day back and you have dinner with your father. We can talk about this later tonight. You didn't have another dream last night, did you?"

"Surprisingly, no. I slept great. How are you feeling?"

Hayden's eyebrows drew in. "I'm fine, why?"

"I just thought since you'd be going back to school today, I don't know, maybe you'd feel uneasy?" I took a bite of buttered toast Hayden had left out for me.

He looked at me curiously, with a half-smile.

I continued. "It's high school, not hunting down ghosts. The same way I would feel uneasy about hunting, maybe you feel that way about high school?"

"That's very thoughtful of you, Ana. But no, as long as I am near you I could never be uneasy."

"You technically don't have to go. I know I wouldn't if I didn't have to."

He laughed. "Yes, I am well aware of your skipping tendencies, but you know why I am going. Luke, on the other hand," he turned his head towards Luke, obviously still angry about last night, "doesn't *have* to go."

"Uh, yeah I do. I've never graduated before."

Hayden scoffed. "You have been tutored your whole life. You've had enough credits to graduate since you were twelve!"

"Yeah but I have never gone through all the formal stuff. What do you care anyway?"

"I love how all-of-a-sudden you care so much about going to a mortal high school when a month ago you would have fought me just for mentioning it."

"Things change, brother," Luke looked at me and winked, "things change."

I rolled my eyes. "Speaking of school, we'd better leave now if we don't want to be late."

Hayden still watched Luke with a clenched jaw. I kissed him on the cheek. "C'mon."

It was my first day back at Ecole since Katrina. Slowly, students and teachers had started to return and the school was now officially open. Ecole, thankfully, didn't suffer that much damage from Katrina. Some other schools had fared a lot worse. Nikki and Marie met me at my locker before class. I was glad at least *that* remained the same.

Nikki frowned when I opened my locker. "You're lucky you had nothing in it, Ana. I had mine all decorated and had to throw everything away. Gah, I hate mold!"

Marie put an arm around her. "We'll help you get new stuff."

"I know, I just had pictures up of us," Nikki sounded truly sad. "I won't be able to get those back."

I looked around the hall; it was empty of any familiar faces. "Where is everyone?"

"A lot of people haven't come back yet." Nikki looked in the direction of my glances.

"Really? It's been over two months."

"I know but, I mean, look at what we have to deal with: flood damage, and now we have to share books? I don't blame them."

"Share books?" I felt totally lost.

"Uh yeah, we lost a lot of books because of Katrina. Plus because of what happened to the gym, we lost half of the football team."

"We didn't lose everything," Marie added.

"What do you mean?" I was dazed, still taking in all the new information.

"There are a lot of new faces from some other schools."

"Yeah, not so friendly faces either," Nikki agreed.

"I feel like I have no idea what's going on. Not only does it feel like the first day of school all over again but it feels like a completely different school." I had hoped my decision to return to Ecole was the right one. I had wanted to hold on to this part of my life, to have something normal. Nikki and Marie meant so much to me and I hadn't seen Rachel for a while.

"I know what you mean," Nikki nodded, slumping her shoulders. It made me sad that she was so dispirited. She was always the one that kept us going.

"Look y'all. It will be fine, just give it time. Look how much this city has accomplished in just a couple months. We can do this. We will be back, okay? Let's be glad we have each other at least, right? Isn't there *any* good news?"

Nikki shrugged but Marie's eyes lit up. "At least there will still be Mardi Gras."

"Of course there will still be Mardi Gras. And at least we still have the same schedules. Speaking of, I have to go meet someone before class." I shut my locker.

Nikki and Marie both looked at me with the same devious smile, they thought I was talking about Hayden.

I felt my cheeks start to warm. "What?"

"Oh, nothing you lucky dog. See you at lunch?"

"Yep. See you later." I told them over my shoulder as I walked toward class.

My morning classes went by quickly and painlessly since Hayden was in my classes. At lunch, Nikki and Marie met me in the commons and we all ate together with Hayden and Luke. It was the first time we all publicly hung out at school together and I couldn't help but feel giddy about it. Just a few months before, Nikki, Marie and I were just admiring the mysterious Boudreaux brothers from afar. Now, a lot of students were watching us, probably wondering just what had happened since Hurricane Katrina.

"Ugh," Luke threw down a garlic dipper in disgust. "Remind me why we aren't hitting up Brennan's for lunch?"

Nikki and Marie giggled thinking he was joking. There were still enamored by Luke, and I knew it would take some getting used to before they were all comfortable around each other. I smiled in good nature but Hayden gave him a hard look.

Luke shrugged harmlessly. "Not even take-out?"

Nikki and Marie— okay, and I—laughed harder.

Hayden must have replied because then Luke said, "Well, if I'm going to have to eat, it may as well be something decent."

"Luke..." Hayden warned.

He pushed himself to a stand. "All right, all right. I am going to head off to my favorite class." A smile threatened his lips. His next class was AP World history, which was one of my classes with him. Hayden had wanted to switch into *all* my classes, but he didn't for the same reason he and Luke split them up: to not look suspicious. I thought back to the first day of school when Hayden was originally in none of my classes. I had even pretended I wasn't disappointed. Then, Hayden had switched into my first three classes. I remembered how odd it was, but I was confident he wouldn't be sharing the rest of my schedule as I'd had AP and two senior-level classes. I had been right: *Hayden* wasn't in the rest of my classes but it came as quite the shock to find that *Luke* was. Who knew my suspicions were right even then? They had switched into *all my classes*; they even came to Ecole because of me. Now, they were staying because of me.

Nikki and Marie left in turns until it was just Hayden and I at the table. I told him I better go early to class to talk to my teacher and, first and foremost, friend, Rachel. I looked forward to seeing her again. She had seemed so distant since everything that had happened. Maybe it was because of the hurricane or maybe it was something else entirely. I remembered how she had first helped me discover the truth about the Lalaurie house. Being a history buff, I had asked her the background to the haunted mansion. *"Stay away!"* she had warned. She was right. That house was evil.

"Ana!" She hugged me and then awkwardly released me as another student entered. She directed me out into the noisy hallway but lowered her voice. "I'm glad you came early today. I apologize we haven't been able to talk much. The internet is still out in our area so if you sent any emails you now know why I haven't responded." She inhaled sharply in brief frustration.

"It's okay, I understand. I have been busy, too, volunteering at Habitat." She gave me a knowing look and I nodded at her in agreement.

"Everyone's been stressed around here, even the pharmacies are out of stock on anxiety meds. I just don't want to lose sight of what's important," she added.

I thought back to my dreams and had a moment of zoning out.

"Everything okay, Adriana?" Rachel's voice brought me back to reality.

"Yeah, it is, sorry." I blew out a breath.

"How's your dad?"

I wished this time that my biggest problems were my father.

"He's fine. Same old, same old." I hadn't told her that I had moved out, or that I lived with Hayden and Luke, for that matter. There was so much she didn't know, which was ironic considering she used to be the only person I told everything to.

"You know, there was a fire at the Lalaurie mansion…"

Where did that come from? "Oh, really?" I spoke coolly. Now I wasn't just keeping things from her, I was lying.

Seconds passed. As she searched my face for something, more students entered her classroom. "I just thought you'd like to know since I recall you asking about the house before," she finally said.

"Oh, okay. Thanks. A lot of buildings were damaged from the storm," I said, changing the subject.

"I know a lot about New Orleans history. If you ever need any information, just let me know." She turned and I nodded at her, taking a step to follow her into the classroom.

She stopped and turned her head back toward me, "and the damage wasn't caused by the storm, Adriana."

My heart stopped. She definitely knew something was up. I shouldn't have kept things from her in the first place. I should have told her everything, and maybe she could have helped me, helped us. I walked in a trance to my desk, resolving on discussing this possibility with Hayden later.

Chapter Four

❖

W hen school let out, I had an exact replica of my dad's truck waiting for me. Hayden or Luke must have brought it for me at some point during the day and I found myself dreading meeting my dad for an early dinner. I checked out the truck; it was in better shape than the original. I hoped my dad wouldn't notice. But it was not like he could object. He got the better deal out of this.

A feeling of sadness came over me, being in the truck all alone. It brought back so many memories and now I was giving it up. Even though it was not a place I would want to go back to, I felt like I couldn't let go. What was worse was knowing that Hayden drove all the way to Texas to buy this truck. For me. And what was I doing while he was gone? I felt like I had gone behind his back, doing a Hunt of my own. With his brother. Who was in love with me. Could my life get any more complicated? My phone on the seat buzzed against my thigh.

"Hi, dad."

Hey, we'll have to find somewhere else to eat, New Orleans restaurant is closed.

"Really? They're still not open?"

Nope, I drove by there after work. Where should we go instead?

He is leaving it up to me? Well, as long as it wasn't Wayne's, where his girlfriend worked...

"I don't really care, dad. What *is* open?"

Let's go downtown. I'm sure we'll find something there. That's closer for you anyway.

"Okay, sure. I'll just call you when I get there. Give me about fifteen minutes?"

K. See you soon.

Brief moment of awkward silence. "Okay. Loveyoubye."

I hung up before he could say anything else. I couldn't believe how awkward it had become with my father. It was like we were strangers. Even when I went over to the house to get random things I'd left behind, it was like I had never even lived there.

I texted Hayden on my drive toward downtown.

> Me: **I must say, nice job on the truck! Its way nicer than the old 1. If he could, my dad would thank you. We changde restaurants, New Orleans is closed :(Eatin dwtwn. Ill call when Im done. Xoxo**

I smiled as I got his response almost instantly.

> Hayden: **Adriana Alexander, are you texting while driving? Call me.**

I couldn't help but smile as I hit 'call.' Hayden picked up after the first ring.

So you are *driving. Your multitasking skills never cease to amaze me.*

"How did you know?"

Your spelling errors and abbreviations gave you away.

"Darn. Well there's no need to worry, I'm an excellent driver."

You know I will always worry. And that's what every driver says before they get into an accident. Plus, I would much rather hear your voice than read a text.

"There are dangers in talking while driving as well," I pointed out with a smile in my voice.

Yes, but at least your eyes will be on the road and you won't be distracted.

"Simply hearing your voice is a distraction."

Do I need to come pick you up before you even make it to dinner with your father?

I laughed, enjoying this playfulness between us. "Then he'd really be suspicious about the truck." I paused. "Do you think he only wants to get together with me because he wants his truck back?"

No, how could you say that? He is your father, of course he loves you. Who couldn't love you?

My mother, I wanted to say. But that wasn't fair. I didn't know if she'd died or simply up and left.

"Oh- I'm almost there so I have to call my dad. I'll text you when we're almost done, okay?"

I hung up the phone with Hayden as I entered the downtown area.

Ten minutes and two closed restaurants later, I sat at a Mexican restaurant waiting for my dad. He'd said to go ahead and get a table—for four. I guess I shouldn't have been surprised that he would bring his girlfriend and their baby. He was with them 24/7, so it would be unthinkable to ask for him to spend any time with me alone.

Finally, my dad arrived fifteen minutes late. "Carla's driving the car back so I can take the truck," he said as he sat down, as if offering me an explanation.

I gave him a closed-lip smile. My smile widened as the cute bundle of baby was strapped into the highchair.

I cooed at Brittney before asking Carla, "How old is she now?"

Carla pulled her reddish-blonde hair over her shoulders and smiled at me in surprise, "Nine months old, can you believe it?"

"She's cute," I agreed to no one in particular.

"She would love it if her big sister would come over and play with her every now and then." Carla's bone-thin hand brushed through soft baby hair.

Carla had children from a previous marriage and at first I thought she was talking about one of them.

I stood gaping at her but the waiter arrived ready to take our order before I could think up a reply.

We talked about babies, storm damage and school while waiting for our food to come. Then my dad got down to business. "I wanted to ask you something."

I shook slightly to unglue my expression and grabbed a chip from the red basket in front of me. "Okay, what is it?"

My heart sped up and I could feel the extra blood rush through me. What was he so nervous about asking me? Something about the truck? About Hayden or Luke? Maybe he just wanted a babysitter? I relaxed a little.

He grabbed a chip and dunked into the dish of salsa before eating it. "Well, it's been pretty tough at work." He spoke around a mouthful of chips. *Oh no.* I hope he isn't asking for any money. I know what he thinks about Hayden and Luke, I mean, he has seen their house. *Kill. Me. Now.* I haven't worked since Katrina except for volunteering. He wouldn't be interested in what I had left in my savings which meant he figured I would borrow from Hayden. I couldn't imagine asking him, after everything he'd done. If my dad only knew how much he had spent on his truck!

"You want money?" My eyes were wide in disbelief and hope he would say no, because I knew I couldn't if he asked.

Carla looked slightly embarrassed and my father adjusted his position in his seat. "What? No." He swallowed a bite of chips. "No, work is good. There's just a lot of it."

"Oh." My dad worked at a salvage diving company, and I suppose they would be packed-busy since the storm. I still did not understand what he wanted to ask me.

"A lot of folks haven't returned since Katrina. And, well, I was thinking you could come work for us 'til things settle down a bit."

"At Taylor Diving?"

"Yeah, c'mon when's the last time you dove anyway?"

I picked at another chip. "I don't know, dad. I just started back at school, between that and volunteering with Habitat..." *and discovering my psychic abilities.*

"It would only be part-time. We really need people."

He said it in a way that left me little room for argument. He didn't care what else I had going on. He wanted this and he would get it.

"Fine." I let out a breath. Here's to more father-daughter time. I sipped my ice water.

"Great!" He set his hands down on the plastic table cloth in relief.

I frowned, not completely understanding why he wanted me to work so badly.

"You remember Mr. Christian? I'll tell him you'll be by after school tomorrow and you can go from there."

"Tomorrow?"

"Yeah, tomorrow why? You don't have plans do you?"

I searched my memory hoping I would find something that I was supposed to do with Hayden or Nikki even. "Well, no but—"

"Okay, then. The sooner the better."

I rolled my eyes. "All right… and yes, of course I remember Mr. Christian. But why? Where will you be?"

"Carla's gotta work tomorrow. They're short at Wayne's too."

Okay, so scratch the father-daughter time. He didn't want me to work *with* him, he wanted me to work *for* him. And now I had already agreed. I couldn't make any objections without Carla thinking I was trying to take time away from them. I felt like I was walking on egg shells around her.

"'Kay," was the most indiscriminating comment I could make. And I spent the rest of the meal not saying much but still walking on eggshells. Carla kept asking me questions about my life and she was especially interested in Hayden. I felt more inclined to open up since she asked about him. She was being so nice but I couldn't tell if it was fake or not.

My Dad and Carla had to get going as soon as I took my last bite of enchilada. I walked them out to the parking lot and was still talking with Carla as my dad instructed her to meet him at home and left. I happily helped buckle a sleepy Brittney into her car seat, struggling with the complex straps until Carla stepped in to take over. She invited Hayden over for dinner sometime and I agreed, wondering if it was an empty request. I watched her leave and turned to my car, realizing that the car I'd had, my dad just left with. I had completely forgotten that I was supposed to text

Hayden for a ride. The darkness at night without the usual street lights was beyond eerie. It was just another thing we had to go without since Katrina. I quickly pulled out my phone to call Hayden.

Hey, you done already?

"Sorry I completely forgot I didn't have a truck anymore, even though I saw my dad drive off with it. Goodbye 'Ol' Red,'" I sighed.

Don't worry about it. Now you have 'old black.'

I laughed. "Yeah right, there is nothing about that sentence that is true. It's definitely not old and it's not mine. And black? Yeah, it's more of a charcoal."

Do you want your own? I could get you your own.

"No, Hayden, that's not what I meant. Anyway, where are you?" Something caught my attention. "Should I meet you out front in ten minutes?"

No, I am here.

"What?" I was startled, looking around the street for his car.

You know I couldn't risk leaving you alone.

"So you have been watching me this whole time?"

I could hear him smiling. *I like how you look when you're talking to me.*

I scoffed at him. "You could have had dinner with us, ya know?"

No, you needed that time with your dad, but I guess you weren't alone after all.

"Yeah, well, you could have at least told me." I saw his car pull out in front. "Far away but always close, huh?" His smile split into laughter. "Well now you will just have to wait for me. I want to run in somewhere real quick." I watched him from outside the car.

I saw his eyes darken. *Where?*

I pointed across the street, nowhere in particular, hoping he wouldn't see the 'Ghost Tours' sign. He looked and then turned his attention grimly back to me. He rolled down the window and I put my phone away, walking towards him.

"What are you doing, Ana?"

"Nothing, why?" I feigned innocence. "I just want to check something out."

"Then I'll go with you."

I leaned through the window and gave him a quick kiss. "I will just be a minute."

I ran across the street, looking back at Hayden with a smile, and pushed a worn wooden door open. A bell chimed and the door shut creakily behind me.

"I'll be right with y'all!" I heard someone yell from the back.

I looked around at the brochures and different artifacts displayed on the counter. There were copies of maps of the tour route and I folded one up and tucked it in the back pocket of my jeans. The place smelled like incense which reminded me of Sansha's house of voodoo and her deliciously devious potion I drank. I inhaled sharply, hoping this wasn't like her house in more way than one.

"Can I help you?"

I jumped as a woman suddenly appeared behind me, breaking me out of my memories. I exhaled a breath of relief as I appraised the woman. Her brown hair had lost its luster, her skin was dry and fingernails brittle and there were tiny creases around her eyes. No, she wasn't like Sansha at all. She had all the signs of aging and stress. She had all the signs of being human. "Sorry, I was just looking."

"Let me know if you need anything, then."

"I'm surprised you're open. I don't suspect you've been getting much tourism." My fingers toyed a souvenir on the shelf as I kept pretending to look around.

She shrugged with all the confidence in the world. "I've lived here my whole life. Ain't no storm going to close me down."

"Here's to hoping there will be more visitors in the spring during Mardi Gras." I moved on to the books, ironically picking up one about New Orleans haunted mansions.

"I hope so. There's been a lot of unexplained events since Katrina. You can't wash away evil, the storm just pissed evil off. So you interested in a ghost or vampire tour?"

I laughed a little, knowing a couple months ago I just had my own personal tour. "No, I was just interested in some information."

"I see you picked up the pamphlet on the Lalaurie Mansion. What do you know there was a fire there about a month ago."

"Really?" I spoke nonchalantly, not trying to show too much interest.

"Yeah." She eyed me and her eyebrows furrowed briefly.

"Well, I have what I need. Thank you so much for your time." I tried not to show panic as I straightened the stack of books and turned towards the exit.

"You're welcome, although I didn't do much."

The bell rang as I pushed the door open.

"You come back and I'll give you a free tour sometime, ya hear?" she yelled from behind me.

I turned and nodded hesitantly before the door shut. I ran back across the street to where Hayden waited.

"Did you find what you were looking for?" Hayden was sarcastic as I hopped back in his car.

I felt the map in my back pocket. "You could say that." I smiled up at him.

"You know, it's insulting that you go to a ghost tour place when I know more about the New Orleans Underworld then anyone here." He was back to being playful.

"That only does me good when you're willing to answer my questions." I played back but he could sense the seriousness in my tone.

He started the engine, pulling away from the curb. "Where is this coming from?"

My heart could have stopped at how easily he read me. *Luke,* I wanted to say. "Nothing. I just feel like I don't know anything about you as a Hunter or what it's like."

"This is coming after spending the evening with Luke, I presume?" He sighed. "That's not who I am. That has nothing to do with the person I am."

"I know, but I just want to know everything about you." I slid the back of my index finger across his smooth cheek.

"You know me, Ana, you are the only one who does."

His green eyes looked hungrily into mine and I forgot about everything else. I did know him. I knew all I wanted to know.

Chapter Five

❦

I was fast asleep that night when I sensed I wasn't alone. I sat up in my bed with a gasp. Upon seeing the figure sitting at the end of my bed, I pushed myself as far as I could backward until I hit the headboard.

"Who are you?" I asked the woman wearing a full wedding dress, sitting at the edge of my bed.

"I'm Christine." Her voice was high, much younger sounding than she looked.

My eyes darted to my bedroom door, waiting for Hayden to sense she was here and burst in at any moment.

"Hayden won't be coming."

My heart dropped at her words.

"Why not?" My throat tightened as I asked.

"Because this is a dream."

I looked at her. "A dream?"

"Of course. I am dead, after all."

"What do you want from me?"

"Just to show you something." She stood up, her skirts ruffling. Her white dress was feminine and elegant. She wore a lace cap with flowers on either side above her ears, the veil cascaded down her back. Dark waves peeked out from under the cap. Her makeup was bold: dark red rouge on her lips and thick eyeliner on the upper lid. Her vintage look reminded me of a pinup girl. She was very pretty and sweet looking, but as she said herself, she was dead. And I wouldn't let appearances fool me. The dress was sleeveless and when she turned, I saw it dipped low in the back, the sash around her waist tied off with a bow. She turned back to me, holding out a delicate hand, "Come with me."

"No."

A small laugh escaped her. "Silly, I was being polite." She swirled her hand and the room started to swirl with it. When she stopped, we were no longer in my room, and I was no longer sitting. I was barefoot in an overgrown courtyard of the French Quarter. "It is not as if you have a choice, dear." She smiled, seeming genuine even though her words were not.

"Fair, enough. I suppose just telling me what I need to know would be too easy for you people," my voice dripped with sarcasm.

"*You people?*" Her delicate face scrunched up, perplexed.

"Yeah, you know. You ghostly, supernatural types."

"Well, you *are* obliged to listen to my story."

"Is it a sad story?" I asked, hoping this wouldn't be a nightmare and not able to imagine how she would be involved.

"Murders always are."

That sent chills through my body, and suddenly the quaint courtyard seemed dark. "Where are we?" I asked, not recognizing the peeled-paint building.

"Pirate Alley."

I followed her as she started walking out of the courtyard to the alley. Nothing looked familiar.

"This isn't—" but then I looked to my right and saw St. Louis Cathedral and Jackson square. "That's impossible. There was a book store just over there."

She started walking towards Chartres Street and my curiosity caused me to continue to follow her.

"Whoa!" It was when an old Model T car sputtered by that I realized we were not just in a different place, but a different time.

"I suppose we should start with the back-story."

I unintentionally hid behind her as a group of men and women passed by. I was still barefoot in pajama bottoms and a tank top, feeling grossly out of character among the tailored suits the men wore and the beautiful dresses and hats the women sported.

"Don't worry," Christine said, "they can't see you."

Because it was a dream. "Right."

"So let's start at the beginning, shall we?" The laughter of the group faded as Christine swung her hand again, and I found myself a few blocks away on a bank by the Mississippi. I swayed, feeling disoriented from the abrupt change in scenery. Cool, wet mud squished between my toes as Christine began talking. "Night seemed to bring out all walks of life. On the Vieux Carre, it mattered not if you came from old money or came to the city from the Bayou. Here, you did what you wanted and wore what you wanted." She paused and suddenly we were next to the street car tracks, with no wave of her hand as a warning. The sand from the tracks stuck to the mud on my feet and everything began to feel entirely too real. "The warm weather allowed many nice girls to try out shorter hemlines and haircuts." We were whisked away to port side, where dozens of ships were docked. I realized by then that she was showing me New Orleans through her eyes. "By day, the Quarta' was filled with the working class, artists and grocers alike. The smell from the docks overpowered fresh baked bread on any good morning but at night everything was glamorous. Even the wealthy came down from upriver to partake in what it had to offer. Speakeasies were common enough and no one seemed to be bothered by them." When we suddenly showed back at Pirate Alley, I, used to her mode of transportation, hardly blinked an eye. "New Orleans had money;" she said as we walked down Chartres Street, "it was the richest in the South. No one troubled themselves with Big Dreams about New York City when you had New Orleans, and with better weather too. It was 1927 when a grand theatre opened up, as did the dreams of many young girls in New Orleans. But only one girl was able to land the lead role in the opening play that year." We had crossed St. Peter's Street when she stopped in front of a building. "And that girl was me."

The sound of an alarm going off startled me. "What is that?" The noise got louder. "What is going on?"

"We are out of time." She looked sad. Her red lips curled down. "*Ana...*"

I could hear someone calling my name but couldn't figure out where it came from.

"What does this all mean?" I hastily asked her. "What is going to happen? Tell me!"

"We'll see each other again in—" and then I was pulled away from New Orleans in the 1920s, pulled away from smells and the neglected building, pulled away from finding out what would happen in the future. If I saw the future in my dreams, why had I dreamt of the past?

My eyes adjusted to the bright light of morning. Someone had opened the curtains in my room and I groaned. I always kept them closed—I loved having it dark in my room. The alarm I heard in my dream was still going off and I looked toward my nightstand through fuzzy vision, realizing that it was my alarm clock.

"Ana. Ana, wake up."

Hayden.

I propped myself on my elbows and tried to clear my vision by blinking. I saw Hayden at my bedside, looking at me with worry.

"What's wrong?" I asked.

"It's time to leave for school. Your alarm clock has been going off for twenty –five minutes. You wouldn't wake up."

"Oh," I said remembering my dream and how real it seemed. I felt as if I was actually there in 1927, seeing New Orleans how Christine had seen it. And I could tell she loved New Orleans then, just as much as I did today. I felt a little smug knowing what I had experienced. I was worried, though, about romanticizing it. She did say she was dead, and she did say there was a murder. "Okay, I'll hurry up and get ready." I nodded, having no real intention of hurrying.

"You okay?" Hayden looked at me from the doorway as he started to leave so I could get ready.

"Yeah. Yeah, I am," I nodded and stood to a wobbly stand. "For now."

"Coffee?"

I smiled, he read my mind exactly.

Thirty minutes and two cups of coffee later, we arrived at school. I was yawning and it wasn't even first period. It felt like I hadn't even slept that night. It felt as if I'd spent the entire night awake. I wished I would only have those kinds of dreams when I didn't have to get up at the crack of dawn for school the next morning. To top it off, I had to work after school. *Thanks, Dad.* That meant I would have to put off deciphering my dream. Until later.

Chapter Six

⚜

After a very long and tiresome day at school I prepared myself for an even longer night at work. Hayden pulled up in front of Taylor Diving for my first day at my dad's job. "You should just get a job here since you insist on driving me," I joked with him.

"Mmm, I would love to but they would find it suspicious if I was diving without gear."

My eyes widened. "Really? You can do that?"

He laughed. "I can but I won't."

"But how? That's not humanly possible."

He raised an eyebrow at me.

"Oh, right. You're not human."

He nodded once.

"That means you don't have to breathe?" I turned toward him, putting the pieces together.

"Ana…"

I threw my head back, my throat exposed. "You always do this. Why won't you just tell me about being a Hunter?"

"Because it doesn't matter."

"It does matter, whether you like it or not, it is a part of who you are. And I want to know you. *Every* part of you." I had changed my mind about knowing all I needed to know about him. I knew what was important, but would my curiosity let that be enough?

"It's not who I am, Ana." His voice softened as he looked at me. "But I get why you feel so inclined to know who I am. You were betrayed by people you didn't know. You have a guard up and it's important to you to know someone really well before you let them in, even a little. You don't know your mom and when you thought you knew who your dad was, he abandoned you. I am just thrilled that you chose to trust me, to let me in."

I felt my jaw drop open a little. "Do not psychoanalyze me, Hayden. How could you make this about me? We were talking about *you*, don't change the subject." My breathing increased in response to my rising anger. He was talking about me, and he nailed it. I didn't like to hear the truth, or so my dad told me on more than one occasion. Still, we were talking about him, and I would think if I was going to be with him forever, that I'd have a right to know just what I was getting into. Why did he keep closing down every time I asked about Hunters? I learned more about it from Luke; he was always open with me, he practically flaunted it. Then it hit me. *Pride.* "You're ashamed," I exhaled in realization.

He closed his eyes briefly and his jaw muscle twitched. "Of course I'm ashamed. I know I can't be who you need me to be."

"You are everything I need you to be." Little did he know that I was afraid I couldn't be who he needed me to be. Could I be like Hayden's mom, Elizabeth? Could I be immortal? I shook my head to clear those negative thoughts. "I love you." I said my last thought out loud then turned to open the car door.

I could hear Hayden sigh from inside. "Do you want to know who I am?" he asked before I could shut the car door. "I am not really living. Everything about me is an illusion. I eat, but I don't have to. I breathe, but I don't have to. I sleep, but I don't need to. Everything about me is an act to make me appear human. For you. Even my heartbeat. The same heartbeat that you love to listen to while lying on my chest at night, the heart beat that puts you to sleep. The only reason I keep it beating is because of you. Is that what you wanted to hear? Have a good day at work, Ana."

The door slipped out from my fingers and shut as the car sped off. I stared at the car in shock as it disappeared into the distance. What, had I hoped that Hayden would sit in the car and wait until I had finished work? I certainly had a lot to think about; Hayden was pissed and revealed more about himself than he ever had before. The things that I loved about him were illusions? No, I didn't believe it. I loved Hayden for who he was, not his body. If I was upset about it, that would make me shallow. I laughed awkwardly to myself; yes liking someone because of their *human* traits is shallow. Nevertheless, I couldn't deny that it bothered me. Hayden made me feel whole, he made me feel normal. That wasn't an illusion, was it?

I walked across the docks absentmindedly until I got to the warehouse that contained the dive shop. My dad picked a great day for me to start working. My dream, my sort-of fight with Hayden, it would all have to wait. And I would have to endure the next few hours agonizing over it, dissecting our conversation, deciphering the dream.

"Hello?" I regretted the nervousness in my voice as I called out into the empty warehouse.

"In here," a small voice answered. I followed the sound as I stepped into a makeshift office.

"Mr. Christian," I felt my relief as he came over to give me a hug.

"Hey, Adriana. How you been, sweetheart?"

"Oh, you know…" I stated ambiguously, not sure what kind of information my dad gave up to my uncle-like friend.

"Well I appreciate you comin'. Lord knows we've had a lot to do since 'It' hit us."

"My dad didn't tell me what exactly you need me for."

"Here, have a seat." Christian cleared papers and dusted off a small folding chair, then went around to sit on the other side of the desk. "Besides the usual inspections, there is salvaging and cutting down wood pilings."

"Okay, so what do you need me to do? Answer phones?"

"A true comedian, Ana. You know your father didn't answer no phones. Plus you have more experience than most of the new temporary guys we got."

I groaned quietly. If I was going to be scuba diving, that would make for a long day. "Whatever you need, Mr. Christian. Just remember, I have school in the morning."

"That's my girl." He smiled. "Come on. I'll show you 'round the shop." I followed him as he led me out into the small warehouse that shelved equipment, hoses, air compressors and jet pumps.

"Your dad's dive hat is in the locker. Everyone is responsible for their own, so make sure you check it before going out. I'll put you in boat inspections since that is least time-consuming, as you'd put it." He winked at me.

"Boat inspections? Why would I need gear for that?" Christian would have to know that I didn't know as much as my dad probably let on when he convinced him to hire me.

He laughed, drawing his smile up so much his eyes were only slits. "You have to go underwater to do the inspection. It's cheaper to hire a diver than to dry dock the boat. That's where we come in."

Metal clanked together in the distance followed by the sound of muffled curses.

I looked at Christian alarmed. "What was that?" Mysteries were no longer my thing.

"Zack, get in here!" Christian called to the other side of the warehouse.

A boy jogged over and slowed as he reached us. "Yeah, dad?" He was annoyed, clutching his right hand in pain.

"Dropped a compressor again? Where are you manners? You remember Adriana, right?"

Zack was in the same grade as I was but he looked younger. Maybe I just felt older. I had seen him a few times at random get-togethers with family. Zack gave me a once-over. "No, sorry don't think I do." He had a boyish, all-American look though his mouth was anything but.

"Oh stop. Y'all used to love to play together when you were younger. I remember when…"

"Dad," Zack whined.

"Okay. But really, she'll be taking over some of her dad's shifts. Why don't you show her around and then Adriana, get suited. You have to be out on the docks by 1600."

1600? What time was that again? I swallowed and managed to nod as I took in the array of new information. *This is not what I agreed to, Dad* played in my mind.

"That's five o'clock." Zack said to me as Christian walked back toward the office. "You should have what you need in your dad's locker. Umbilicals are over there." His hand dropped before I could see the direction he pointed in. "See ya." Zack walked back to where he came from. Something told me he either wasn't too happy to see me or wasn't too happy to be interrupted.

"Oh and Annie?"

"It's Ana…"

"We go by military time here so you better learn it."

"Thanks for the advice!" I yelled back. Geez, what was I, a magnet for jerks? Typical teenage boy. And he was always so nice around my family. Although I'd hoped for a little more direction on what to do, I couldn't blame him for not wanting to train me. I knew exactly what it felt like to have to work for your father. In his case he was really working for his father, I was just working in place of my father.

I nervously went through all the inspections on my equipment before putting on my wet suit. It felt like years since I'd last dived, not months. I hoped I wouldn't screw up too badly. After I was suited, I stood around looking like an idiot until Zack came and got me and dragged me out into the chilly Mississippi. I didn't know what he expected me to do, and I was ready to tell Mr. Christian that I couldn't do this and my dad would have to find someone else. That was until my head submerged underwater as I lowered myself deeper into the river. I had almost forgotten the serene feeling of being weightless underwater and it was exactly what I needed right then. I was lost in thought with nothing but the sound of my breathing and the vision of cloudy water when Zack tapped me out of my reverie. I tried to read his eyes but they showed neither disappointment nor annoyance as he signaled me to follow him and watch what he was doing. My fears of screwing up were eased by the time we had finished. It wasn't as hard as I'd thought and if this was all I had to do then I was in luck. The boat we were working on was huge and definitely a two diver job. We had to have our dive hats on for this one, and Mr. Christian was up top monitoring our surface air. I cleared my mind and tried to pay attention as much as I could, knowing on the smaller boats I would be diving by myself. And I realized I really didn't want to let Mr. Christian down. This was his livelihood, and if I didn't know what I was doing now, I'd better learn fast. When Zack and I had surfaced, he confirmed that he just let me watch this one but the next time he would actually expect me to work. I shrugged, past caring, and feeling relaxed after being in the water.

It wasn't until I saw Hayden's car pull up that I realized for the past few hours I had forgotten all my problems. Having time to step back and look at our little disagreement, I saw it for what it was; inconsequential. And maybe I had overreacted from the combination of stress and lack of sleep. When his car finally stopped, I almost ran into it to apologize. I gripped him into a hug and exhaled the day away.

"Long day?" He laughed, obviously already past our earlier conversation, and seemed to enjoy my possessive hold on him. "Who's that?" he asked when I finally let go.

"Who?" I turned my head out the window to see who he referred to. Zack stood outside the warehouse, smoking a cigarette of all things, glaring at us. I drew my lips up as I was reminded of how he treated me after the dive. "Oh. That's Zack, Mr. Christian's son. I had a really long day. I just want to forget about it right now."

He leaned in and gave me a chaste kiss on the lips, then shifted gear. Soon work was long behind me, both literally and figuratively.

"You don't have to work, you know. You don't have to want anything ever again." I knew where he was going with this and noticed he deliberately left out any mention of money. I knew he had money, but it didn't matter how much; I refused to live off of him.

"It's not even about that. I'm not just working to make money; I'm working to help out my dad and Mr. Christian. They are so busy as it is and I don't blame him for not trusting the expensive temps."

"You always worry about other people. When are you going to do what's best for you? You are already volunteering and going to school full time. And let's not forget you have premonitions you have to deal with. You've been picking up your dad's slack for too long."

"I know you're just trying to protect me, but it's not even about my dad anymore. After seeing Mr. Christian today, well, he is like family. He took care of me when I was just a baby and now I am old enough to help and he needs it. I want to be there for him."

"I love your heart, you know that?"

"I love yours." I smiled back at him and tried not to show the frown that threatened when I remembered what he had told me about his heartbeat.

"Let's just relax at home tonight," he sighed. "I'll even cook." He laughed sweetly.

"You always know how to make me feel better, do you know that? How about this: I'll go home and start making my grandma's red beans and rice that you love so much and you can go get us a movie. Deal?"

He gave me a brilliant, boyish smile. "How can I say no?"

Chapter Seven

❧

Hayden dropped me off at home so I could get started on dinner. I was still smiling as I took my shoes off in the mud room. The thought of Hayden picking out a movie was amusing. It was something so normal. I thought about how easily he could pull off both worlds. Like he fit perfectly into both while I, on the other hand, didn't fit into either.

The rest of the house was dim and I thought it was safe to say Luke wasn't home. I hated how I was unconsciously keeping tabs on him, though I felt relieved he wasn't there. The way he lingered when Hayden and I spent time together had become awkward. The last time we watched a movie in the living room, I caught him watching us from his laptop. From there on out, Hayden insisted we watch TV in my room. I didn't argue with that.

I switched on all the lights I possibly could; I figured being relieved of fearing the dark justified wasting energy. I went into the kitchen and immediately got started on the beans. Going for the speedy version of red beans and rice, I used the presoaked, canned ones. I worked quickly, getting out the cutting board and a big pot.

I opened the refrigerator to grab a few ingredients, half expecting not to have what I needed. I was still getting used to not living with my dad. Going from nothing to everything is not something you can get used to overnight. It used to be a constant aggravation to round up money for groceries or pull something together besides cereal for dinner. Sure enough, the fridge was stocked full. It was always full. I thought back to how Hayden didn't need to eat. He did this for my benefit and it wasn't until just then that I realized how much he did for my benefit. That made me love him even more, but also question how much of his true nature he was hiding. Did he feel like he was missing out? Was he holding himself back? I pushed stupid thoughts away and concentrated on dumping the beans in the oversized brass pot.

I stirred them into a mixture of jalapeños and water when Luke walked into the kitchen from out of nowhere.

Luke chuckled at me being so jumpy, then spoke, "Hey, Ana."

"Hi Luke…"

"Why do you say it like that?" He noisily scooted out a bar stool and sat down.

"I am just trying to figure out what you want?"

He chuckled devilishly again. "Oh, there are so many ways I could answer that."

"You know what I mean," I cut him off. "What's up?"

"Nothing. I just wanted to be with you. Be in here with you," he quickly corrected. "Hell, Ana, I just want to be around you."

"Luke, this has got to stop. I'm not going to keep hanging out with you if you're going to keep trying to…I don't know, seduce me? Here, chop this up." I handed him a cutting board with an onion on it. He took it but looked at it questionably. "I value our friendship. Please don't ruin that."

He stared at the onion and I smiled, imitating chopping it. He shrugged and grabbed the biggest knife from the block on the counter.

"Fine, I'll stop. For now. But just hear me out. Don't do anything drastic, like *bind* to him. That means you're stuck with him for eternity." He rubbed his eye with the back of his hand.

"I'm young. I haven't even graduated yet. I have no idea what I am going to do tomorrow let alone next year. I'm not even thinking about that."

"You don't think I get that? The thought of being with someone for eternity scares me too. But with you—everything makes sense."

"Spending eternity with someone you love doesn't sound so bad. I love Hayden, I wouldn't be here without him. Literally. Or did you forget you wanted to kill me?"

He chopped the onions angrily and then pushed the cutting board toward me. I gave him a saccharine smile as I took them and stirred them into the beans. He let me cook in silence for a while, shaking his head every so often. He cocked his head quickly, as if listening to something, then turned back to me.

"You just need to think about a few things first, that's all I'm saying. Just promise me you'll at least consider it. We have so much in common… we're the same age." His voice was low.

I concentrated on stirring. "I'm not 18." I heard the garage door open and I gave Luke a look.

"Funny, Ana. You know what I mean. Just tell me you'll think about it."

I squeezed my lips into a line waiting for Hayden to come inside. I flinched as Luke tossed the knife on the counter and walked away.

Chapter Eight

❧

"**W**hat are you doing up so early?" Hayden kissed my lips when he saw me the next morning in the entryway tying my tennis shoes. "I thought I'd go for a run before school," I said sheepishly.

"A run?" It was even more embarrassing that he looked surprised. *Okay, I need to get out and exercise more.*

I shrugged. "Yeah, I don't know. I just feel like I have all this energy lately and I just need to get it out. I need to run." I could feel the adrenaline build even just speaking about it.

Hayden looked at me curiously, then smiled. "Okay, I'll go with you then."

"Really? You don't mind?"

"Not at all, I like to run."

"Are you coming because you want to or are you coming because you think you should?"

"I'm not sure what you're trying to say, you are as elusive as ever, but yes. I want to, I'll *always* want to."

I fought a girlish chuckle at his comment while I finished tying my shoelaces. Hayden went upstairs to change. By the time I stood up, he was standing in front of me again.

"I thought you were getting dre—oh".

"I don't like to keep you waiting." He winked at me.

Hayden was effortlessly clad in black shorts and sleek tennis shoes. He wore a sleeveless shirt, his tanned arms perfectly muscular. I couldn't keep myself from reaching out and touching them. I made a mental note to not let him wear anything like that to gym class at school and added jealousy to the list of new emotions I experienced lately.

Our neighborhood was perfect for running through, with a lot of streets to lengthen the route and a pretty path through the golf course. I had wondered why I hadn't taken advantage of it before, when I had lived with my dad.

"For how long have we been running?"

Hayden looked at his watch and answered easily, "about a half-an-hour."

"Really?" I said surprised. It didn't feel like we were running for that long. I wasn't even out of breath yet. "We'd better start heading back."

"School," he agreed.

A wicked smile spread across my face. "I'll race you back."

His dark hair spilled back as he laughed.

I stopped running and put my hands on my hips. "I'm glad that amuses you, but I'm serious."

"Okay, Ana, I'll race you." He fought a smile as he worked to speak seriously.

"No cheating."

"Obviously. It's bright as day with humans everywhere."

"And don't *let* me win, either." I pointed a finger at him in warning.

He leaned toward my face almost touching my nose, "I can't promise that."

I was slightly disoriented when he moved back. I grunted as I turned in the direction of the house. "Ready?"

He nodded once and we both took off toward the house. Even at human speed, he was superternaturally fast. I pushed my legs harder against the pavement, wanting and needing to go faster. The sensation I got when I ran was unlike anything thing I'd felt before. Well, maybe I'd felt it once before. The more I ran, the more it fueled my need to run. Faster and longer. The house came in view and I didn't slow until I got to the front doorstep. I felt disappointed when we stopped.

I bent over, slightly panting, but Hayden looked at ease. "You let me win," I scolded him between breaths.

"I did not."

I glared at him.

"Okay. Maybe I did. I didn't promise that I wouldn't, remember." He winked. "You were fast though, I almost didn't have to."

"Stop teasing me."

"I'm serious, Ana. You were really fast," he said as we walked into the house.

I caught a glimpse of the clock, quickly panicking at the time I had to get ready for school.

"Oh no, I have to shower." I started running up the stairs. "Oh and after school, is it okay if I take the car? I want to run somewhere after work." I turned around when I reached the top.

"It's too soon to be going anywhere by yourself right now."

I put my hands on my hips. "You're being paranoid. It's been months since I've had a death threat."

"How can you say that so casually?"

"How can you not? You're the one who can't die."

"Hilarious," he said sarcastically.

"Hayden," I slowly walked down the stairs, looking up at him through lowered lashes while giving him my best pout, "I'll be fine. It's just work again, around lots of people. Then I just have to run somewhere real quick, twenty minutes tops, and I'll come right home."

He gave me a slighted look. "Where's 'somewhere?'"

"Downtown. Again, lots of people."

His features relaxed, he knew what I was doing.

"Sure, I'll just get a ride home with Luke."

And yet he trusted me.

My heart warmed. I gave him a quick kiss and then ran back upstairs to get ready for school.

As other schools rebuilt, most of the new faces at Ecole left and some of the old ones even returned. Slowly, day by day, piece by piece, we were coming back. I thought back to a couple months ago, just after Katrina, and the words of the naysayers who had told us not to rebuild or that New Orleans would never be the same again. How silly all that sounded now. I still tried to do as much as I could with volunteering. Working at the diving company took more of a toll on me than I had hoped for. I used to not mind working for my dad when it was teaching the scuba class at the St. Bernard Parish community center. Now, and finally, I had a life. I wanted free time.

I didn't know if it was me that had changed or the school, but going to school each day was suddenly different. Knowing Nikki and Marie would be there, and Hayden and Luke, I actually wanted to go, now. The only thing that hadn't changed was Stephanie. Clearly nothing fazed her, not even a Hurricane.

My morning classes, like always, went by quickly and peacefully except that Stephanie had been looking particularly smug since third period.

I looked around my AP history class with the feeling that something was missing. Luke wasn't at his desk and my thoughts directly went to Hayden. Had he skipped as well? Did they have to go take care of something? I quickly texted Hayden before Rachel started her lecture.

> Me: **Hey, where r u?**
>
> Hayden: **In class, without you.**
>
> Hayden: **Why?** He added quickly.
>
> Me: **Just checking :)**

Okay so he was in class and Luke wasn't. So it had nothing to do with hunting. Which meant Luke was absent for his own personal reasons.

I found it hard to pay attention during class. I debated whether or not to do something about my dream when I got off from work. I wanted to go to the theatre.

Late last night, as I lay in bed with my eyes open, I thought about my dream and what it had meant. The theatre had sounded familiar and I knew I had to have passed it countless times while in the French Quarter. I remembered the brochure I had taken from the ghost tours place and wondered if I still had it. I took a chance and dug through my laundry basket. I found the map just where I had left it: in the back pocket of my jeans. Sure enough, one of the highlighted stops was La Petite Theatre du Vieux Carre aka Vampire Street Theater. I flipped the map over a few times, looking for any information on why it was "the most haunted theatre in the South." I seriously considered taking the owner up on her offer for a tour. If I was going to keep having these dreams, at least I should know the history behind the places.

Although I hadn't committed to going yet, there was a pit of excitement and nervousness in my stomach just thinking about it. I couldn't concentrate on schoolwork but rather on going over the details of what I would do if I went. Would I just drive by? Should I ask Hayden to come with me? Should I go back to the ghost tour place? If I kept this up, this would be a long day. And how, exactly, was I going to make it through work?

Rachel lectured almost the entire period which gave me plenty of time for several scenarios to run through my head. I felt guilty for not being able to pay attention to her.

After class, I gave her space and decided not to stop by her desk. Absentmindedly, I got my things and started to leave.

"Adriana, I'd like to talk to you please."

Uh-oh. From her tone, I knew it couldn't be good. Most of the class had already left but a few students turned their heads. It was like being sent to the principal's office; but I wasn't in trouble, was I? I nodded and started walking over to her. I thought back to our conversation yesterday about the Lalaurie mansion. She must have known something and now decided to confront me about it. I sat down in the desk closest to her while she was still sorting through folders in a filing cabinet.

"Hi," I alerted her to my presence, after she didn't seem to notice me. When she just continued searching through her desk I wondered if I had even spoken in more than a whisper.

She looked up at me, her eyelids heavy and a little startled. "I wanted to talk to you about a paper of yours." She continued searching through papers. *Ok, so this wasn't how I thought the conversation would go.* She wanted to talk to me about my academics which made me worry even more. She finally came up from her file cabinet defeated. "Sorry Adriana. I've just gotten tired."

I saw the exhaustion in her face, too, and immediately my concerned instincts took over. "Are you okay? What happened?" It was hard to believe a lecture wore her out. She was so collected earlier; even when she was teaching she was always confident. Her demeanor had completely changed and I couldn't help but think how out-of-character it was.

"Oh, no, I'm fine really." She put a few papers in a manila folder and put a book on the shelf behind her. "I just haven't been sleeping well in general."

"I'm sorry." My apology was genuine, but what else could I say?

"Nightmares," she added quietly.

Now I had a ton to say. "Nightmares? What do you mean nightmares? What kind of nightmares?"

"It's nothing. I've just been stressed about my house. I don't know if I should sell it and just take the losses or not..." her words faded.

Oh. So not *my* kind of nightmares.

"Again, I'm sorry." I put my hand on her desk in an unconscious effort to comfort her. "Is there anything I can do?"

"Oh, I'll be fine. I did my dissertation on the history of dreams. If I am dreaming about selling my house, then that is the path I should take. Dreams aren't just random. They have meaning. They tell you something. So if I am dreaming I should sell my house, I have nothing to lose by pursuing it."

I couldn't believe how great her timing was! Although our nightmares were completely not in the same ballpark, maybe not even in the same country, she was right. I had nothing to lose by pursuing them. I already knew my dreams were telling me something. They certainly weren't random, now I just had to figure out what exactly it was they were trying to tell me. And that meant that I was going to go to the haunted theater after work. I smiled at her in silent agreement.

She seemed pleased that we came to the same conclusion. She looked up at the clock on the wall. "You'd better get to your next class."

I looked at it, too, briefly forgetful that I had a schedule to follow. When I saw that my next class was about to start, I scrambled out of my seat.

"You're right. Thanks. We'll talk later?"

"Always," she promised.

Before I was out the door, I remembered something. "Oh, I almost forgot, you wanted to talk to me about a paper?"

Her drooping eyes were now wide, "Yes, but I was mistaken. It was another student's paper."

I looked at her with confusion, until she gave me a reassuring smile.

"All right, then." I bowed my head and walked out. *She definitely knows something's up,* was my last thought before I went to gym.

I walked to my locker after gym, noting rather irritatingly that Luke was, yet again, absent. Then I worried that Hayden wouldn't be able to get a ride home from him. I would either be late to work if I had to drop Hayden off at home or Hayden would be driving me. I texted him to meet me at my locker, hoping he would have an explanation about why Luke was gone.

"Hi," he kissed my cheek. "I thought you were going straight to work from gym. Can't stay away can you?" he teased.

I gave him a patronizing smile. "Ha-ha. No, I *was* going to leave but—"

"You ready to go?" Luke interrupted us, his backpack slung over his shoulder like he was here the whole day.

"Yeah, one second. Did you change your mind about me driving you?" Hayden didn't turn his attention from me.

"No, it's ok. I just wanted to say goodbye."

"Bye," Luke clipped. *Ugh, what was his problem today?*

"Not goodbye," he cupped my face, "see you later." He rubbed my lower lip with the pad of his thumb, leaving me breathless. He winked as he walked away with Luke. Stupid work. Stupid dream. There were many things I could curse. And I did just that on my short drive to work.

Before I even walked into the shop, Zack came out of the office. "Suit up; you're going to actually work today."

"Hello to you, too." I tilted my chin up.

Seeing Christian at his desk, I ignored Zack's order and walked into the office.

"Hi, Mr. Christian."

"Hey baby girl." His sweet southern drawl was a contrast to the bitterness of Zack's.

"Busy today?" I asked, wondering why Zack wanted me to get suited up right away.

"Yeah. 'fraid so."

"More than usual?"

"We've got boat inspections all week, on top of the salvaging. I had to send half my boys off shore on those Gulf jobs. They won't be back for another week."

"I see." And I officially felt guilty for having the weekend off.

"Dad, I need that compressor," Zack was behind me, speaking in a slightly more polite tone to his father.

"Well, come get it." He tilted his head to the right of him.

Zack drew his lips in and raised his eyebrows as he went to take an air tank. He hesitated, fiddling with the valve.

"Don't worry about it though, Adriana. I got your dad coming in and we got Zack here."

"Oh and Dad," Zack jumped at the opportunity, "since we have an extra body, I was hoping to get Friday off."

"Friday off?" Christian spoke the words as if they were inconceivable.

I slowly started to back out of the office.

"For what?" Christian added.

"There's just something important I want to do. Friends, ya know?"

"Not this week, Zack. Ana's dad isn't coming in to replace anyone, we need him and we need you."

Zack exhaled, clearly unhappy about not getting Friday off but not saying so. "You don't understand..."

"I can work for you!" I blurted out before I could think it through.

Christian's head shot up. "Adriana, no."

"No, it's fine really. I don't mind." That wasn't entirely true, but I considered it my peace offering to Zack. I hoped he would go a little easier on me if I did this. That wasn't the only reason, though.

There was something about what he said that reminded me of myself. I didn't work twice as often as he did and it still was enough. He was a teenager. He wanted to go out and live his life. He wanted to be normal and he was right, his dad didn't get that. How many teenagers worked full time? How many were scuba divers with more responsibility than most adults?

"No!" Zack's bellow broke through my thoughts.

"Zachary…" Christian scolded him.

Zack ignored his father and turned towards me. "No. I don't need you to work for me and I don't need your help."

"I'm sorry, I just…" I tried justifying my offer but Zack had already left. *What is with everyone today?*

"Sorry about that, Adriana. I'll have to have a good talking to with that boy later," his voice carried the threat.

"No, please don't. It's fine. I was just trying to help."

"I know you were. You always are. That's the problem, ain't it?"

How right he was. "Yeah, well I'm going to get suited up. I take it I'll have the honor of being Zack's dive buddy for the inspection on that ginormous boat on our docks out there?"

"'fraid so," he spoke his classic saying with a little humor.

I sighed. "Bye, Mr. Christian."

There was only one locker room, so I took the gear out of my dad's locker and headed to the bathroom. I was putting on my wet suit when there was a knock, no, a pound, on the door.

"Hurry up."

"Yes, Zack." I only had so much niceness left in me. I hoped one day I wouldn't snap, because it would not be very becoming when it finally came out.

Zack kept the rest of our conversations clipped and professional. I was thankful for at least that. But what was *he* mad about?

I was the one who tried to do something nice for him so he could have Friday off. He should be thanking me not blaming me. The only displeasure he verbalized was a grunt when I said I had to leave for the night. Apparently, he had to stay and do the paperwork. I didn't allow myself to feel bad about it. I had a haunted house to check out.

I texted Hayden that I would see him soon, and then started toward downtown. I had passed the theater countless times in my seventeen years or so of living in New Orleans but I'd never been inside. I circled the theater on St. Peter Street a few times before finding a spot in which I didn't have to parallel park. After sliding in next to a meter, I cut the engine. *Now what?* I inhaled, afraid to think of the answer. I already knew what I was going to do. Based on the signage, the building was still used as a theatre and therefore open to the public. I didn't know if I should feel relieved or chilled to discover I could go inside. Relief was what I settled on when I stepped out of the car. The aroma of food in the air was almost masking the mold and mud smell left by Katrina .

I walked around the terra cotta colored building until I found a set of doors that wasn't shuttered. The theatre was two stories; a balcony with identically shuttered doors was above me. I peeked into the window panel, resentful that there wasn't more activity going on inside. Do I just go in or should I knock? It wasn't exactly show time, but I figured if the door was unlocked, it permitted entrance. When I turned the knob, the creak of the old wood was the only barrier to it opening.

Inside, the lobby was huge and opened up into a courtyard. There were two separate theatres on either side. I looked in both directions.

"Hello?" I softly called out.

I sucked in a breath and walked toward the courtyard. *Where was everyone?* The late afternoon sun shone through into the courtyard. 1960's style tropical wicker furniture scattered the courtyard as did a mix of flora from palm trees to ferns to carnations. A squawk from a bird flying overhead broke the silence as did the sound of water trickling from the fountain. All together, I felt as if I were in utopia. I spun around, admiring this little piece of paradise in the Quarter. *Seriously, where was everyone?* My heart pumped at that realization. A door above slammed from behind me and I turned around with a jump. I looked up to the second floor balcony, trying to see if I could see anyone inside the French doors. I was nearly on the tips of my toes, squinting my eyes and preparing for what could possibly appear in the windows of those doors, when the sound of splashing made me turn around again. The frantic splashing came from the fountain. I swallowed, my heart beating wildly in my chest. I did not have a good feeling about discovering what was making the noise. It sounded completely unnatural. I took a few steps toward the fountain and peered over. My lips quivered open as I let out a gasp. Inside the fountain was a dozen Koi, swimming wildly about. All I saw were blurs of orange and shimmers of white as they jumped around. Swimming as if they were trying to flee. I was entirely unsettled by that thought. What explanation could cause them to behave like this? I looked around, remembering this theatre was haunted. Did animals react strangely to supernatural beings? Could the fish sense a ghost was near? I whipped around, feeling as panicked as the fish.

"Christine?" My voice shook, just taking a chance and hoping it was her. *Hoping it was just the friendly, wedding-dress wearing, murdered ghost who haunted my dream? Really, Ana?*

"Can I help you?" A male voice called out from the second floor balcony, sounding as if I wasn't supposed to be there.

I exhaled a breath of relief and held a hand to my startled heart. "I'm sorry, I was just looking around." I shielded the sun from my eyes and looked up at the thin, twenty-something man with dark, parted hair and thick rimmed glasses.

"The theatre is closed to visitors except during performances. How did you get in?" Again his voice was suspicious and scolding.

I apologized again. "I didn't know. The door was open so I just thought it was okay to come in."

His arms were holding the railing and I could see him relax a little. "Pauline must have left it unlocked again." He shook his head and muttered admonishingly to himself. "Stay right there. I'm coming down," he ordered.

"Okay." I was starting to feel like he was right; I shouldn't be there.

I heard him coming from behind me and I turned to face him. "I'll just be on my way…" I pointed my thumb over my shoulder towards the exit.

"Why did you say 'Christine?'"

"Did I?"

"Yes, you did. You called out her name just before I spoke to you." His shoulders were squared and he was not buying my feigned innocence.

"I—" I really didn't know how to answer that. *I thought I felt the presence of a ghost so I called out the name of the murdered actress who brought me here in my dream. Oh and I can see the future in my dreams.* Probably should come up with another explanation. "This theatre was on the ghost tour map and I was just curious about why."

He nodded, like he determined I was harmless. "So you're a tourist looking to catch a glimpse of Christine, the infamous matron that haunts our theatre?"

"That's right," I agreed.

"Well then you'll know this isn't where you're likely to see her."

I smoothed my fingers through my hair. "I'm afraid I'm not really familiar with the tale. Maybe that's why I came?"

"Are you a journalist? You look awfully young."

I let out a good-hearted laugh. "No, just curious."

He looked at me pointedly. "Well, I'd hate to take business away from any of those tour places but how 'bout I tell you the story as I walk you out?"

I nodded curtly. "All right." I found it a little amusing he didn't trust me to let myself out.

As he walked me out, he painted a much grimmer picture than Christine had. Christine *had* landed the lead role in the play that year, but never made it to perform. Right before opening night, she was found dead in the courtyard from having fallen to her death. An understudy reported that he and Christine were drinking and doing—ahem— other things, when she lost her footing and tumbled from the third story balcony. She was still dressed in her costume from that day's rehearsal, which explained the wedding dress she wore in my dream. Okay, so she wasn't a jilted bride.

"So, it was an accident?" I asked as another thought occurred to me, when Christine had said she was murdered.

"Of course. Like I said, drinking was involved and she never could have survived the impact on the flagstone courtyard. Why do you ask?" He was back to his previous suspicious self as he opened the front door to let me out.

"No, reason." I stepped out into the sunlight. "Thanks for the information."

He gave me a pensive smile. "Sure." The door shut and I heard the click of the lock as soon as I turned toward my car.

Chapter Nine

❧

"**S**tephanie, what are you doing here?" I was shocked and a little disgusted to come home and see Stephanie sitting on *our* leather couch. She looked more dressed up than what I was used to and her silky hair was perfectly straight.

"Oh, hello Ana." She smiled almost sincerely. *Ha*, I knew better than that. I thought over all the possibilities as to what could have brought her to our house.

"Are you selling cookies?" I added with some sarcasm. It was better than asking her what the heck she was doing in my house.

"Ana? What are you doing here?" Luke entered the living room from the kitchen, two glasses full of sweet tea in his hands.

"Um, I live here?"

"I know but I wasn't expecting you back so soon."

"What is going on?" I looked between the two of them as he sat down on the couch next to Stephanie, handing her a glass of sweet tea in my favorite Turvis tumbler. They started talking, laughing even, and appearing as if they were picking up conversation on which they'd previously left off. "Hello?"

"Oh, I am sorry, Ana," he stood up as if to make introductions. "You remember Stephanie? She is in my grade?"

"Of course." I gave her a short smile. "Um, Luke? Can I talk to you for a second?"

"Sure, what's up?"

"In the kitchen please?"

He set his tea on the coffee table. "Be right back." He smiled sweetly at Stephanie.

He followed my lead to the kitchen and when I thought we were out of earshot of Stephanie, I turned around to face him. "What is *she* doing here?"

"Why do you care?"

I opened my mouth to speak but realized I couldn't answer that. Why did I care? Maybe because it was Stephanie, the very epitome of a snob.

"I am free to do whatever I want, Ana. I live here, too. I don't mind when you bring your hyper friend what's-her-name and the other quiet one that always stops breathing when I am around."

"That's different…"

"How is that different? Because Stephanie is interested in me? It's not like you're my girlfriend. You chose Hayden, remember? I will be around for eternity, might as well have fun with the girls who *are* available."

"Is that why you brought her here? To make me jealous? C'mon Luke, what are we in, 2nd grade?"

"Why, *are* you jealous Ana?" He had a devilish smile.

"That's ridiculous!" I felt my cheeks starting to get hot and knew I had to change the subject. "And what's with the 'I didn't expect you back so soon?' I get home at the same time every day after diving, don't play dumb."

He struggled to find his words, "I guess I was just having such a good time with Stephanie that I lost track of time."

I shook my head in disbelief. We stared at each other for another minute or so.

"Now, if you'll excuse me, I have to get back to my date."

"Date?" I asked to his back.

"Why do you care, Ana?" he reminded me as he exited the room.

"Rrg." I grunted at his impossibility when I heard Luke and Stephanie pick up their conversation again. But he was right. Why did I care? In one way or another I had chosen Hayden. I loved Hayden. He was more than I could ever dream up. But why was I so bothered with Luke going out with Stephanie? I thought back to all that I knew about Stephanie, from the years of high school we had together. And then every memory of her cruel acts surfaced: her spreading rumors about girls I knew and liked, the name-calling, the fights, the boyfriend-stealing and so much more. Yes, Stephanie was not right for him at all. Anybody else would have been fine, but her? Why *her*?

Chapter Ten

✤

I left the house and called Hayden to tell him we would be going out that night. The reason: there were pests in the house. He took me seriously for a moment, vowing to call an exterminator. I laughed at the thought.

I didn't know what time Stephanie had left my house that night, I was just relieved they were both gone by the time we returned.

When we got to school the next morning, I had hoped that Luke, maybe even Stephanie, if that's who he was with, wouldn't show up to class again. Hayden left me at my locker, saying he had to go take care of something and I knew that 'something' was talking to Luke. I shut my locker, turning the dial to reset it and walked up to Nikki and Marie talking in the hall.

"This is going to be so fun, I'm glad they decided to still do it this year."

"What's going to be fun?" I asked, dreading what kind of event they'd drag me to next.

"The Mardi Gras Parade and Masquerade Ball," Marie replied as Nikki dragged me a few lockers down to look at the poster on the wall.

"Like you don't know." Nikki could always fake looking offended.

I glanced over the poster that was bright with the purple, green and gold Mardi Gras colors. Every spring, Ecole had their version of a spring homecoming, complete with royalty that got to ride on the float during the Mardi Gras parade and a masquerade ball the following night.

"So, what are you so excited about? We didn't do the ball last year. What, are you running for Queen?" I joked with her.

"I know, but it's different this year," Nikki was totally serious. "And as a matter of fact we were just talking about who should be Queen."

"Who *is* going to be queen or who *should* be queen? Because *Stephanie* and *anyone else* are two different things."

Marie laughed but Nikki wasn't giving in. "No, but really, we think you should run."

"You're kidding."

"Uh, no we're not. You should definitely do it."

I turned away from the poster and shook my head. "You know I'm not into those sorts of things…"

"Why not? This is Mardi Gras were talkin' here. Put your animosity for organized school events aside and think about the true meaning of this. You stayed positive even when I wasn't. Look at all the things you've done, like your volunteering and helping clean up. You never lost hope in New Orleans."

"You really are the heart of New Orleans," Marie nodded. I looked at her in surprise and thanks.

"See? If Marie says it, then it's true. You have to run for Queen."

"Who's running for Queen?" Stephanie and her entourage stopped in front of us.

"None of your business," Nikki belted.

"Oh 'hi' to you, too, Nikki." Stephanie batted her eyelashes. "Ana…" she looked at me, gloating in the fact that she had been with Luke. In my house.

"Hi, Marie. Well, look at you. Did you lose weight?"

"No…?"

"I know," she frowned fakely. "I can tell."

"Okay, that's it—" Nikki raised her fist and I held her back.

"Come on Nikki, let's just go." If anyone was going to hit Stephanie, it was going to be me. But words can sometimes wound better than violence.

"Oh, and Stephanie?" I turned back as Marie and I were pulling Nikki away, "Me."

"You? What are you talking about?" Stephanie's lips curled in disgust.

"*I* am running for Queen."

The three of us walked away, laughing while we heard gasps from Stephanie and her friends who always stood by idly. Priceless was seeing the look on Stephanie's face.

Shortly after, Stephanie had recovered. In English, she had no reservations about hiding her dislike of me. In fact, she took it out on all those around her. She really did look like a girl possessed. She was announcing to everyone her running for Queen and confirming that they, of course, would all be voting for her. I tried to lose myself in Hayden, but Stephanie's gaze kept flicking towards us.

"What's going on?" Hayden asked quietly. I was glad that Hayden could sense Stephanie's hostility. At least he had sense, not like Luke.

"It seems I am running for Queen."

Mr. Atkins interrupted our conversation with the announcement of a pop quiz. Everyone but Stephanie stopped talking.

"I'll pass out the test once I see everything is off your desk and you've stopped talking," Mr. Atkins announced the last part loudly, looking at Stephanie. "You have fifteen minutes to take the quiz. Good luck."

I looked around the room. Everyone seemed to be dreading and worrying simultaneously. Everyone except Hayden. Of course, he would do well. He probably knew the material better than Mr. Atkins. I tried to push aside the worry that came over me from this realization.

"*Stephanie*," I heard someone whisper. I looked up to see who would be whispering to her for help. It wasn't one of Stephanie's usual clones. I had seen her trying to be a part of Stephanie's circle before but something told me they weren't the welcoming type. "*Stephanie*," the girl whispered again, a little louder. Stephanie looked at Mr. Atkins who read the newspaper at his desk then back at the girl, irritated.

"Yeah?" she hissed.

"I forgot my pencil case. Could I borrow one?"

Stephanie and her friends fought giggles. "Guess you won't be getting an *A* this time." Stephanie turned around in time for Mr. Atkins to look up and shush the girl. I hadn't started my quiz yet, in shock at what I saw in front of me. How could Stephanie treat someone like that? Someone who, despite all Stephanie's internal ugliness, wanted to be her friend?

I dug through my bag to find a pen, then quietly stood up on the other side of my desk and leaned forward enough to drop the pen on the girl's desk. She turned around to see who had done it; I just gave her a quick smile, sat back down and started taking the quiz. I didn't need a thank you. It was what any normal human being would do.

I could feel Hayden radiating beside me. Despite my best efforts to hide what I had done, nothing went unnoticed with him. I looked at the girl again. She was smiling, my pen moving wildly about as she was hard at work on her quiz. She looked so innocent. Funny how there were people as good as her in the world and those as evil as Stephanie. They almost balanced each other out. Almost how Hunters balanced the Underworld against evil. Except in this world, those like Stephanie ruled it. And those like that girl, wanted to be like her. How backwards things could be.

Chapter Eleven

❧

I left Hayden in the hall to go to my next class, which was one of my classes with Luke. Luckily, I made it there before him and couldn't care less if he showed up today or not.

Luke sat in the desk next to me. I ignored him, pulling out my notebook and concentrating on the board ahead. I was *officially* mad at him. It was one thing for him to keep giving me a hard time about being with Hayden, but it ticked me off that he was with Stephanie. She was evil. Couldn't he, who killed demons with his own hands, realize that? And now I had to run for Mardi Gras Queen because of him. Or her. I didn't know whose fault it was but I had already gone through every possible scenario to back out of it and it wasn't looking good.

"Hey, Ana," Luke called from beside me.

I pressed my lips together.

"The silent treatment, huh?" He was amused. "Maybe I deserve it? At least I know now you *are* jealous."

I whipped around to face him, "I am not—"

"Could everyone pass up their assignments from yesterday, please?" Rachel started the class and Luke chuckled softly. He knew just how to push my buttons. I passed my assignment to the girl in front of me. "Today we will be reading out loud about the fur trade and then answering the questions after the chapter." I looked away from Luke as Rachel collected the papers in the front row. "Thank you to all of you who did the research yesterday, despite lack of books. We will be working in pairs today as we only have enough books for each pair to get one, so I apologize, but, with hope, working together will make it go quickly."

Students started moving and turning their desks. I felt a desk bump against mine and the all-too-familiar, alluring scent assaulted my nostrils.

"Partner?" Luke raised his eyebrows at me and I stared back at him, my blue eyes to his hazel.

I shook my head fervently. "Oh, no. I don't think so."

Luke looked a little disappointed but recovered. "Well, too bad. Looks like you're out of luck." The words were laced with venom.

I looked helplessly around the room, and he was right. Once again, I was stuck being his partner. I stared him down, shooting daggers at him.

Rachel came by and dropped a book on my desk; the sound caused me to lean back. What was going on with her? We definitely had a lot to sort out later.

"Do you want to record or should I?" I asked, flipping the pages of the book to the correct chapter.

He was taken aback by my tone. "Um, I can."

Yeah, now he tried to be nice.

"Ok, first question: What states were most impacted by the North American fur trade, and why?"

I flipped forward through the chapter making sure I had the correct answer before having him write it down.

"What are you writing?" I looked on nervously as he scribbled away on our paper.

"The answer," he said obviously.

I rolled my eyes at him. "Let's just pretend you don't know all the answers this time. I'll tell them to you and you can just write, okay?"

"Whatever."

"Okay, next question—"

"If I do this for you, will you at least listen to me?" I hated how his eyes looked almost vulnerable because this good side of Luke was even more dangerous to my resolve.

"What? No. You think by helping me unwillingly cheat on the assignment, I should reward you?"

"It's not cheating since I already know the answers."

"You know what I mean. We are supposed to look them up. *Together.*"

His smug smile returned. "Together? I like the sound of that."

"Well, you'd better get used to liking the sound of it with Stephanie. Maybe you two are perfect for each other after all." I pointed my pencil at him. "Okay now, on to question two."

He sighed and I was skimming a paragraph when a torn piece of paper slid in front of me.

Why are you mad at me?

I looked up at him and smiled. "What, are we in 2nd grade?" But I couldn't resist replying.

Anything I say is going to make you think I am jealous. I'm not mad at you for dating. I'm mad that it's Stephanie. You know we don't like each other- is that why you chose her?

I pushed the note towards him and continued trying to read about fur trading in North America. A second later, another note blocked my view.

If it was anyone else, I wouldn't get a reaction out of you. Plus, why not? I don't see anything wrong with her. She is obviously interested in me. At least someone is.

You and I are just friends. so what you do is none of my business but please keep the trash out of the house.

Ha ha. Ouch. Didn't know you had it in you Ana. Me like.

You have no idea what I am capable of. But seriously. I don't trust her. If you insist on dating her, don't bring her to the house. I live there too ya know.

I heard him fight a chuckle as he scribbled something on the piece of paper.

"Okay, that's enough." I crumpled up the note he handed back to me. "I've said what I had to say. If you want to continue a civil relationship, please respect that."

"Anything for you, Ana." And I hated how serious he sounded. I really didn't know how to act in front of Luke anymore. I cared for him, but I loved Hayden. I couldn't keep allowing him to make me question that. Yet every time I tried to pull away, he just pulled me back in. I shouldn't make a big deal about it. I should be able to act normally with my boyfriend's brother.

As the class ended and I was putting my notebook back in my bag, I noticed someone hovering beside my desk. My head shot up to find an unfamiliar face.

"You're Adriana, right?" A girl I didn't know was in our class spoke.

"Yes? I'm sorry, I didn't catch your name?" Sitting in the back, I hadn't noticed her before but she was beginning to look familiar.

"I'm Bailey. Do you volunteer at Habitat?"

"Yeah. I don't think I've seen you there - do you as well?"

"Not really." She smiled sheepishly. "My church group dragged us out there one time. I think it's great that you do, though." At first I was hesitant about why she was being so nice to me but she sounded genuine and just as wary as I was.

"Oh, well thank you." I slung my bag over my shoulders and stood up.

"I should be thanking you," she said after I thought our conversation was over.

I looked at her quizzically, waiting for her to explain.

"For helping me out in English. Stephanie didn't have a pencil so..."

Oh! It was the girl I gave the pen to in English. My mind was so busy thinking of other things that I didn't put two-and-two together. "You don't need to defend Stephanie. I'm sure she had plenty of pencils. She knew what she was doing."

Bailey nodded in realization. "I don't know why I let her push me around. All I used to want was to be her friend but today I was so humiliated; I probably would have not even taken the test if I'd had to ask someone else for a pen." She looked off to the side, thoughtfully. I couldn't imagine why she divulged all this information to me. She was nice, but wasn't she afraid I would use it against her? Did she feel like she could trust me? I started to tell her goodbye as I noticed Luke was waiting patiently at the door.

"So, I heard you are running for Queen?" Bailey added as I made my getaway.

"My friends kind of made me do it, but I am warming up to the idea." I smiled as we walked together toward the door.

She looked at Luke, and her breathing hitched in intimidation. "Well, you have my vote," she managed to get out in one breath. Luke smiled charmingly at her and she fled.

"What was that about?" Luke bumped my shoulders as I walked to his side.

"Why do you care?" I reminded him.

He tipped his head back in laughter then he bowed, holding his arm out for me to walk through the door. "My Queen…"

Chapter Twelve

❖

I woke up screaming. Again

My worst nightmare had just happened. Literally. I had always complained that I had never known who the people were in my dreams. I guess the saying, "be careful what you wish" for is true. So many people. So many familiarities. My first instinct was to cry, but then I realized it hadn't happened yet. I still could keep it from happening. My eyes shot open and the rest of my body followed. As I sat up, I looked around the room for something familiar. Hayden wasn't in sight. I grabbed my phone, nearly ripping it off the charger as I started to write to him.

> Me: **I hope you are just
> down stairs.**

I doubted it but sent it anyway.

> Hayden: **Good morning to you, too.
> I take it you haven't
> had your coffee yet?**

> Me: **Funny, but seriously.
> Where are you????**

Hayden: **Iss everything ok?**

Hayden misspelled a word. I must have over done it with the three question marks.

Me: **Sorry, everything's fine here. Are you on a Hunt? Why wouldn't you wake me to say goodbye?**

I could picture him wincing as I typed the word Hunt.

Hayden: **Yes, Adriana. I'm finishing up now. And I did kiss you goodbye. A lot. I tried to wake you but you were out cold. Tell me what's going on?**

Something dropped in my heart. I had that kind of nightmare and I couldn't even wake up from it? That is beyond unsettling.

Me: **I had a really bad nightmare last night. Luke Hunting Mr. Christian. Please get home now.**

I waited a good thirty seconds before I received his reply.

Hayden: **On my way.**

As I waited for Hayden to come back, the details from my dream haunted me. I replayed it in my mind at least ten times. With all certainty, I was sure. Luke would kill Mr. Christian. It would happen only three days from now, at the masquerade ball. I could see the dress I was wearing, the music they were playing.

And Luke. Killing. Doing what he does best. With his bare hands. I ran down the stairs before I knew what my feet were doing.

"Luke, I need to talk to you."

He glanced over his shoulder before turning his head back to the television. "I hope you're not going to school looking like that."

My lips pressed into a hard line. I was too worried to be hurt by his words.

"Ana, I'm kidding. You know you never look less than perfect." He sighed and went back to the TV. "You're beautiful," he mumbled.

"I need to talk to you. Now." I put my hands on my hips to feign authority. I heard the TV click off but I didn't look away from him. He got up slowly, drawing it out just to get a rise out of me, relishing in his position that I finally wanted something from him. *How dare he?* I was irritated but only because I knew I wouldn't get him to listen to me. Surely I would have some hoops to jump through. Didn't he see that this was serious? This wasn't just another hunt, this was someone's life—a human's.

Before I knew it, he was right in front of me. His head cocked to the side, he looked at me trying to gauge my emotions. I quickly changed them—anger, urgency, fear—that's what I wanted to project. Seriousness.

A lazy smile crept over his face. "You wanted to talk to me?"

I regained control of my thoughts, "Yes. It's about a dream I had. Come on, let's talk about this in the kitchen." I turned back when I noticed he wasn't following me as I walked toward the kitchen. Once again, he showed me I was at his will.

"If it's another adventure you want, all you have to do is ask." His lazy smile got a whole lot more sinister.

102 · JENNA-LYNNE DUNCAN

"No, Luke. That's not what I meant. Please, let's talk." Again, I turned toward the kitchen.

"Fine," he relinquished. He lightly caressed my arm as he spoke. "Tell me about your dream. I'm glad you came to me about it." His look was genuine and it hurt me for what I was about to tell him next.

I opened my mouth to speak but the front door whipped open, slamming against the wall. "Ana!" He called out and then lowered his voice as he saw me in front of him with Luke. "Is everything okay? Did you tell him?" Hayden looked worried.

"Um, no. I..."

"Tell me what?" Luke interrupted. He looked at Hayden and then back at me. The realization dawned on his face. "So you wanted to tell me about your dream because I had something to do with it?" He was mildly angry.

"It's not what you think. In my dream, you were on a hunt but who you killed was human." I got the words out, hoping I would make sense.

"So that's what this is — an intervention?" Now he was more than mildly pissed. "You called Hayden here because, what? You couldn't tell me yourself?"

"She was worried. Who you killed wasn't just a human; it is someone she's close to."

"I was talking to her, not you Hayden." Luke didn't take his eyes off of me. "Answer me, Ana. You called Hayden before you even came down to talk to me about it?"

Called, texted there's a difference. I wondered if I should push this white lie. I sunk my teeth into my lower lip, knowing that I couldn't. Luke was always straight forward with me. "I did."

Luke bowed his head.

"Just listen to me. My dream took place at the ball at Ecole. For some reason, a Hunt leads you there. And for an even more unknown reason, you killed Mr. Christian. My boss, my dad's friend, and my uncle for all intents and purposes." I took a step toward him. "I don't want a repeat of what we already went through; please just promise me you'll stay away from the ball."

Luke took a step back. "I'll do what I want, Ana."

I looked at Hayden, who up until then had been giving us space and allowing me to explain. "Hayden?" I pleaded for him to help. That was a mistake.

"Hayden? What the hell can Hayden do? Have you ever thought that maybe you can't change the future? Ever thought that you're just dreaming it before it happens? That you can't actually do anything about it?"

Tears started to form in my eyes, but I refused to wipe them away, refused to show him that he hurt me. The one person that had trusted me, believed in me, now doubted me.

"You're just saying that. You believe in me. What about the jogger? We saved him."

"Believed. Past tense. And what about the jogger? We didn't actually see that he made out alive."

I felt the air leave my lungs. "You're just trying to hurt me. You don't mean it." I had to take every ounce of dignity and strength I had left to keep myself from crying and running away. I fought hard my instinct to run, I would not do that again.

"Oh, like what, the way you hurt me?"

"That's enough, Luke." Hayden stepped between us. "Just listen..."

"I don't have to do anything! You are not in control of me. You can't keep me from the ball, even though I know that's what you'd like, *Hayden*. Anything to eliminate the competition, right? No. I'm going to the ball. And I'm going with the only person I want to go with: Stephanie."

"Luke, please listen. I'm trying to help. Not only for Mr. Christian's sake, but for yours. I care about you. " Luke's lips parted and I could see him easing up. Then I spoke, "You're my friend."

"I don't want to be your damn friend!" Luke looked right at me, rage in his beautiful hazel eyes. The tension was building up and I didn't know if I could take it anymore. Before I could decide what to do next, he turned and stomped out toward the garage. Seconds seemed to trickle by as I heard the engine roar and tires screeching away.

I felt Hayden's warm embrace as he pulled me back against his strong chest. I melted in his arms, signaling something only he could understand.

"It's not true, Ana. You can change the future. You can help people."

"I hope so." My exhale was laced with doubt.

Chapter Thirteen

❧

Hayden told me to go to school and not to worry. His parents were coming to town and this whole thing would be sorted through. This was one of the hardest things I had to do yet: continue to carry out my normal activities like nothing had happened and nothing would happen. I was relieved that Mr. and Mrs. Boudreaux would be coming. I knew Elizabeth had probably missed her boys like crazy; I just wished their visit was under different circumstances. It was about an eleven hour drive from Tampa, which would bring them in late at night. If they chose to fly, there would be a good chance they would be there after school. I wished it were the weekend. I thought about asking Zack to cover for me or calling in sick to Mr. Christian, but I didn't know which option I dreaded more. So, now I would just have to put up with this nagging feeling all through school and work. Worse, I would have to face Christian. Would that be even possible after seeing him murdered in my dream? No, I told myself. That wouldn't happen. Hayden wouldn't allow it, I wouldn't allow it. Even if Luke wouldn't listen to his parents, there would be some other way. But who could really say no to Elizabeth? Or not follow Christopher's orders? There was a reason I'd had that dream, I kept telling myself. That reason was to save Christian.

I stared out the window as Hayden drove us to school. Luke definitely wouldn't be there today. I wondered where he was going all this time? I was conflicted by the thought, wanting him to come back and hoping he wouldn't so there would be no opportunity with Christian. If he left— if he split for good— how would that work? How would they Hunt? What if he didn't Hunt? The thought scared me. Would everyone be destroyed? Luke claimed he loved me. Would I be destroyed? What bothered me the most was that he *had* claimed he loved me, how then could he just change his mind? Would he just leave me like that? Dang it, why did that bother me? He must have been foolish to think I was actually 'the One.' If he could never stop loving me, how was it he could so easily flirt with Stephanie? No, he didn't even know what love was. If you were in love you wouldn't—no, couldn't, think of being with anyone else. Right? Nausea overcame me and I felt myself longing for something else to fill my thoughts.

"What's wrong with you today?" Nikki caught up to me at some point during the day as I sauntered down the hall to another class.

"What isn't wrong with me?" My lips slightly pouted.

"Oh quit the self-pity party. What's going on?"

"You want the good news or bad news first? Wait, never mind. There is no good news."

"Woe is me, woe is me. C'mon! The parade is in two days, the Ball in three, and rumor has it you're the next Queen!" She sung the word queen.

"Yay." The word lacked any tone or emotion.

"Very funny. How is it that you can go through so much, not even Katrina got you down and now something—oh no, it's not Hayden is it?"

I looked at her angrily. "No, never." I wasn't really angry with her, I was embarrassed with myself. What got me down wasn't Hayden, it was Luke. And that I would never admit.

"Ok fine. Geez— touchy, touchy. Change of subject. There must be *some* good news."

I shrugged, unconvincingly. "I know what dress I'm going to wear to the ball."

Nikki cheered.

"I just haven't found it yet."

Her cheering halted. "Then how do you know what it looks— oh." The realizations dawned on her. "Ohhh." She drew out. "I see. Well, no worries. We'll go to the mall, find the mystery dress and then hang out at Marie's after."

"Can't, I have to work after school again."

"Okay, so we'll go after work. You can meet us there."

"Can't again, Hayden's parents are..." I stopped myself, remembering I hadn't told her that Hayden and Luke lived alone. "I have plans with them," I concluded.

"Fine. No time for your two best friends anymore. You have a rich and beautiful new family that loves you. I understand. But I don't think Marie will. She seemed pretty insistent about having us over tonight. I think it's important." Her head dropped to the side and she tried her best to play the sad puppy dog. I knew she was playing me but I couldn't help but feel sorry. "Marie needs us," Nikki added, and that did it for me. I wanted to be there for them.

Christopher and Elizabeth might not even be home by then if they drove. "Fine. I'll meet you at Marie's after work, okay?"

Nikki clapped her hands together, her somber expression immediately forgotten.

"Geez, I just agreed to hang out, not end world hunger."

Luke wasn't at school the rest of the day, like I suspected, and Hayden left after lunch hour to go pick up his parents from the airport. Of course they flew in. It was silly of me to think they would drive. Christopher was close to two hundred years old and probably had more money than God, although he would never show it. And this was an urgent matter; they wouldn't take their time by driving. But I had already given my word to Nikki that I would be going to Marie's and I was starting to really look forward to it even though that meant I would have to wait until late tonight to help them sort out this Luke problem.

I was lucky to be able to get out of work early, vowing I would be doing some serious boat inspections tomorrow to make up for it. I got to Marie's house around dinner time. I thought about bringing food but figured we could just order in if they were hungry. Personally, I didn't think I could stomach anything. The anxiousness just to get there was enough to fill my stomach.

Marie lived with her parents and grandma in the garden district, about twenty minutes from me, although I couldn't recall actually meeting her grandmother. We had hung out a few times in the past year but had only gotten close over the past few months. I suspect I was to blame for that. It took a whole lot of changes for me to realize just what good friends I had. I had transferred to Ecole my sophomore year when the cliques had already formed. I had felt like, and wanted to be, the odd one out. Funny how quickly things change.

I had always admired Marie's house. Who wouldn't want an apartment in the French Quarter? But it was the history that intrigued me. I knew that this building was probably as old as Hayden. I laughed to myself at my attempt at humor.

I passed through the courtyard; the overhead light flickered twice before going out with creepy timing. I found myself running up the stairs to her front door. Her house had a cottage feel, a scaled-down version of a centuries-old bourgeois Creole interior. The furniture was romantic and beautiful, the mahogany furniture you'd expect to find in a place rich of French influences. Hadn't I learned my lessons from beautiful houses? You could not deny the beauty of the history behind them but sometimes that history was dark. And something you should stay far away from.

I was relieved when Nikki answered the door almost immediately after my first knock.

"It's just Ana!" Nikki called into the warm apartment behind her then let the door swing open so I could enter.

"Sorry to disappoint you." I shrugged off my jacket, hanging it on a hook on the wall of the foyer.

"Oh sorry, Ana! I just thought you were the pizza guy. You know how I get when I'm hungry."

The corners of my mouth curled down briefly out of regret. I should have brought takeout.

"Once I get a little slice of heaven from Louisiana Pizza Kitchen, I'll be fine," Nikki vowed.

"Where's Marie?" I looked around the living room noticing she wasn't with us yet.

"Oh, she's in the bedroom setting up."

"Setting up?"

"Yeah go in there, I'm just going to grab some chips and I'll be right in."

"'kay," I replied over my shoulder as I found my way to her room from memory.

"Hi!" Marie said with an excitement and nervousness as I hesitantly pushed her bedroom door open. Candles were scattered in places, flickering the only light across the room.

"What's going on?" I concluded that everyone was acting strangely.

"Nothing. Why do you ask? Come sit down." Her words spilled out quickly, nervously.

My eyebrows were still raised as I dropped my bag to the floor and sat down on the edge of her bed.

"I just wanted you guys to be here for something. Don't look at me like that, it's not a big deal. Okay, so it might be but don't worry."

I sat staring at Marie, trying to decipher her emotions. Nikki ran into the room and leaped onto the bed, nearly catapulting me off.

"Want some?" She held out a bag of chips; the smell of dill pickles assaulted my nostrils.

I shook my head and then turned my attention back to Marie.

"What is it that you wanted us to be here for?" I asked her gently.

Nikki popped a chip in, crunching loudly. "Show her," Nikki said around a mouthful of chips.

Marie drew her lower lip into her mouth.

"Marie…" I warned. The anticipation was killing me.

"It's nothing much," she spoke coolly as she disappeared into her gracious walk-in closet. A second later, she came out backwards, bent over and pulling something across the carpet. A box? When she turned it, it came into view. It must have been heavy if Marie was dragging it and it was most certainly not made of cardboard.

"A chest?" I was incredulously noting how solid it looked. And how old.

Nikki wiped off her hands and came to kneel beside us on the floor.

We waited for Marie to explain. Clearly Nikki already knew what was going on by her relaxed attitude. I was tense; my muscles locked, waiting for the other shoe to drop. It was sad that I was starting to always expect the worst, waiting for something bad to happen.

Marie ran her hands over the wood, feeling the grooves of the design that appeared intricately and delicately carved in. Suddenly, I felt everything was about to change. As she fiddled with the lock on the front of her small chest, I felt something was wrong. Marie spoke before I could express any of my concern.

"As you know, it is my eighteenth birthday in a few days. My granny gave me this chest. It has been in our family for generations. Why she gave it to *me*, who knows. I asked her why she hadn't given it to my mother to keep. My mom has always liked old things; I mean she did save every drawing I'd made since preschool. But she only said it wasn't needed until now." Marie inhaled and exhaled sharply then continued.

"What's inside?" there was more fear in my voice than I realized.

"I haven't opened it yet. I mean, I have my suspicions because my granny has been telling me these stories since I was a kid. I wouldn't normally have made such a big deal about it but something about it just exhausts me. I knew I needed y'all here with me. To give me strength. To find out whatever it is in this box, because I feel like it's important, ya know? I am drawn to it. And I'm scared." Marie trembled and I put my hand over hers. She was drawn to the same box I felt repelled to. I was more curious than ever. Whatever was in there was not just something Marie needed to find out, I was dying to know as well.

"Just open it already!" Nikki blurted out, voicing her shared impatience.

I shot her a slighted look and turned to Marie. "Whenever you're ready."

"No, Nikki is right." And she shoved a single key into the lock and twisted. A heavy click sounded throughout the room and the top of the chest popped open. The smell of sandalwood and lilac filled in the air round the chest. Marie threw the top back and we stared inside in awe.

"What is this stuff?" Nikki asked, not bothering to hide her disgust.

I knew exactly what it was. I had become unwillingly familiar with voodoo since I'd met Hayden and Luke. After they had kidnapped me, they brought me to the house of Sansha, a voodoo priestess. It was there that I saw how real voodoo was in Louisiana, and got a taste of it firsthand. She had given me a potion that was supposed to make me sleep, but instead I had fought the battle for consciousness and stumbled about incoherently as Hayden, Luke and I continued evacuating. I sighed to myself, remembering that was the first time I had kissed Hayden. The potion had given me false confidence, numbing my senses and dulling my instincts to fight or flee.

Now it was all out in front of me. The contents of my memories sprawled out before me in a chest meant for Marie. My memories, my personal history, out in the open for everyone to see. But this wasn't about me. This, for some reason, had a connection to Marie. And why she had a trunk full of gris gris, potions, powders and what looked like a grimoire, was something I was going to find out.

Marie took out the battered textbook bound in some leathery material and held it wearily to her chest.

"No, seriously? This is kinda weird." Nikki picked up a small bone in between her forefinger and thumb before throwing it to the ground. "That was from an animal, right?"

"Voodoo." I answered. "Don't touch that!" I held out my hand to stop Nikki who was about to smell a vile she uncorked. "This is a trunk for a voodoo priestess." Nikki put the cap back on then set the vile back in the chest with wide eyes. I was hesitant to touch anything but Marie was taking inventory. Taking things out of the chest and placing them on the floor beside her. "The question is: why does Marie have it?"

"I don't know." Marie was shaking her head in wonder. "Like I said, my granny gave it to me. For my eighteenth birthday." Suddenly, that sounded so wrong.

As the last of the contents piled out from the chest, Marie shook her head. "They were just stories. I didn't know any of it was real."

I opened my mouth to ask Marie to explain what stories she was talking about when Nikki shrieked and pointed at the bottom of the chest. "I ain't touching it!"

I looked in to see something tightly wrapped in cloth and tied with string.

"If it is a head, I am *so* out of here."

Marie didn't reply, I don't even think she heard Nikki; she was looking at the chest with fascination. Her shaking hands floated toward it slowly and untied the string. She carefully parted the cloth and pulled out a dress.

"That's the dress I'm wearing to the ball." My heart froze in my chest. Marie looked the dress over. An amethyst Victorian-style gown with gold brocade and satin. It was accentuated with matching foliage. When I could breathe again, I reached out to run the tips of my fingers over it. It was a beautiful dress and the craftsmanship was like nothing you'd ever see—in this century.

"I mean *wore* to the ball, in my dream. Of course I wouldn't wear it now." I found my voice but stuttered nonetheless.

Marie's jaw was set and she sat silently staring over the dress and the items from the chest.

"*That's* the dress? The one we were trying to find? How freaking weird is this? I think I have had enough of these supernatural co-incidences to last a lifetime.

"There are no coincidences. Only destiny." Our heads whipped toward Marie, who spoke in a zoned out calm.

"What's wrong Marie?"

She shook her hair out once and then started piling everything back into the chest. Everything except for the dress. "Nothing. Just tell me about your dream."

I didn't want to start talking about my dreams again; it was Marie who needed the support now.

"Tell me," Marie urged with a sense of demand. I hesitantly described to her the ball and the dress that I saw in my dream while she worked to put everything away and slide the chest back into the closet. Of course, I had to leave out the part about Luke killing Mr. Christian as it would give away their secret. A secret that wasn't mine to tell. Even though I had told my friends about my new abilities, I had never told them the whole truth, including that Hayden and Luke were Hunters. After Marie slid the chest back into the closet, she laid a mask on my lap. "This is for the dress."

"Marie. I can't—no. It was just a dream; I don't expect to actually wear the dress. I couldn't care less about what I am wearing."

"Okay, for one, the dress is not going to fit me. And most importantly, when are you going to realize it wasn't just a dream?"

"What are you talking about?"

"For whatever reason, your dreams are predicting the future. That's not supposed to happen. I am not about to mess with what is destined. If it were under other circumstances, I would have opened the chest by myself and found the dress which I would have shown Nikki, who would have said how perfect it would be for Ana to wear to the ball. Then she would have made you wear it and you would have gone to the ball in it just like what happened in your dream. But because I felt something and wanted you here with me to open the chest, and because of what *else* you saw in that chest and because for some reason you are a psychic and saw yourself wearing it in a dream ahead of time, you don't want to wear it now. Well, I'm sorry. You are going to. I don't want to be the one who suffers from the repercussions that come from trying to change the future.

"Are you saying I can't change the future?" Luke's words came back to me. *Do you ever think you can't change the future. You are just dreaming things before they happen.* Hearing them from her mouth made it all too real.

Nikki mumbled something but no one heard her. We were too engrossed with what was developing. Our shoulders squared, hands on our hips, and our eyes locked. Countries have gone to war for less.

"I'm not saying anything; I just don't want to bear the consequences for trying to change the future. I think you should just leave your dream alone and wear the dress as if you never saw what happened in the first place."

My heart sank. Did she know what she was saying? If she knew what really happened, would she be talking like this? Where is this coming from anyway? This was the most outspoken I'd seen her since we'd been friends.

"*Trying* to change the future? Are you saying that I can't? That I can only *try*?" Oh God, please say no.

"That's exactly what I'm saying," Marie huffed. "Now can we just move on to something else?"

"What about innocent people? What if innocent people die? You would do nothing to try to help them if you were me? What about that jogger in one of my dreams who was attacked? Were you not the one who told me where you thought the location was?"

"I told you that so you could get a better understanding of your situation. Your dreams."

"Again, you've lost me. Are you saying you wouldn't try to save someone's life if you had the chance?"

"You can't change what's already written. You can try but it only upsets the balance."

"What are you talking about Marie? Where is this coming from? This isn't like you." It's not that I didn't like this new passion that was coming from Marie but it was different. It was a change. And under the circumstances, a change I wasn't ready for.

"This is me, okay? This is who I am."

Those words were eerily familiar. And at that moment I realized there was something more about Marie that I didn't know.

I took a breath and waited until I knew I was calm. "I don't care who you are — what you are. I just want to be your friend. This night was about you and I'm sorry if I turned it around to me and my stupid dreams again. I'm scared too, you know? I am not ready to believe that there is no reason I'm having these predictions and that I can't do anything to help people. Anyway, we don't have to talk any more about it. *Right now.* But just know I am here for you and you can tell me anything."

I waited, hoping that she would confide and me and talk about what was going on but she just lowered her head and nodded in agreement. I nodded mine and fought hard the urges to press the matter.

"Where's Nikki?" I looked around the room, realizing we were alone.

Marie looked around too but didn't answer. We walked to the living room but she wasn't there. A light shone from the kitchen. Inside, Nikki was slumping over an open pizza box at the breakfast table.

"What's wrong?" I pulled out a chair to sit next to her. Marie did the same.

"The pizza guy was here. I tried telling y'all but I guess you didn't hear me with all that fighting you two were doing. Want some?"

She slid the box in my direction but Marie and I declined. "We weren't fighting. And is there something else bothering you?"

"Nope." She set down her piece of cheese pizza. "It's just…You know I don't like being left out of things."

"Seriously?"

"Yeah, seriously. You guys are all super freaks and I'm just normal. Nothing cool about me."

I placed my palms flat on the table. "Are you kidding? I would do anything to be normal."

Marie pushed her lips together so I continued talking. "Even when I didn't have all this *stuff* going on, I still wished to be normal, to be like you Nikki. Believe it or not, I felt bad all those times you dragged me to the mall and got annoyed with me. I wanted to be like you, *for you*."

She stared at me before a wide smile broke across her face and she started chuckling. "That's really sad Ana, you know that?"

"I know that now. I didn't know that then." I playfully hit her arm when she wouldn't stop laughing. "And you know what? Now I'm happy with not being normal. I wouldn't change it for the world."

"And I didn't get annoyed with you."

"Sure," I teased her.

She straightened, becoming serious. "I didn't. Really. To be honest, I admired you. You just did your own thing and didn't care about what people thought of you. I just wanted you to like me and your indifference wasn't giving me any assurance."

How funny you hear these things when you need them the least. "Maybe that is my problem: not caring about what people think of me."

"Stop, you're fine. Marie why are you so quiet? Don't you have something to add to this sob fest?"

Marie tried to smile genuinely.

"It's okay, Marie has a lot on her mind already." I smiled at Marie who was looking up at me through lowered brows. I shivered unwillingly. "I'd better get going." I pulled out my cell from my back pocket to check the time.

"What? You just got here!" Nikki protested.

"Talk to you later…" Marie and I said at the same time.

Nikki looked over at Marie with confusion and a frown.

"I know but I still have something with Hayden's parents and have to bust my butt tomorrow at work for leaving early today."

"Sure, ye need yer beauty rest, the grand ball is naught but in a fortnight."

I couldn't help but laugh at Nikki's attempt at an accent. "That was wrong on so many levels."

"I'd like to hear you do better."

"I'm just saying, a fortnight is about two weeks. The ball is only two nights from now. And what kind of accent is that anyway? English, Irish? The masquerade ball celebrates Fat Tuesday and Mardi Gras, which have French influences so not only is your geography wrong, but your time period as well."

"Why am I friends with you again?"

I shrugged. "I just like history." My thoughts briefly drifted away from my conversation with Nikki to why exactly I liked history. Had I always been interested in it? Or was it something new, as a result of the events and people around me, that history has began to play such a big role in my life? I thought about Rachel and why she had turned to history. Was there an event in her life that forced her to look into the past? Ironically, the fact that I saw the future was what forced me to seek out the past.

"Why do you and Marie keep zoning out tonight? Geez- I thought this was going to be a fun night but you two are a bunch of downers." Nikki's sarcasm brought me back and I scooted back my chair to stand up.

"Well, I'll see y'all tomorrow."

"Bye, Ana! Can't wait to see you in that dress!"

Marie said goodbye in no more than a whisper and I walked out of the kitchen with a frown that showed exactly how I was feeling.

"Marie, I was just kidding."

"It's not that."

I heard the fading voices from behind me.

I shut Marie's front door behind me, hoping Marie would come lock it after I left. As if I didn't have enough to think over, I now had Marie to figure out. Marie's family obviously has a strong connection to voodoo. How does one become a voodoo priestess? Are they born into it? *Passed on from generation to generation?* And where was I going to get that information from? I told Hayden everything but I didn't know if I would feel right about telling him this. I didn't tell her about him. Once again, it wasn't my secret to tell.

This was the start of my long drive back to the house where the events of what had just happened with Marie loomed and the nervousness of the pending confrontation with Luke awaited.

The only thing I remained hopeful for was that Hayden's parents had been there for hours and probably had already talked some sense into Luke. That, or he had never come back from wherever he went.

I didn't realize how nervous I had become until I arrived home and stepped out of the car. That's when all the blood that had been pumping through me rushed from my head. I didn't notice the extra car in the driveway or the noises coming from inside. I expected to see what I had seen the first time I met Hayden's parents: Christopher's calm, welcoming presence and Elizabeth's warm, caring smile. It was only once I hesitated at the front door that I realized there was arguing going on inside. Four distinct voices; Luke was home.

Chapter Fourteen

✤

"**I** just came to get my things, and then I'll be outta here." I heard Luke in the living room as I clicked the door shut quietly behind me.

"Luke, sit down this instant."

If they had sensed I was there, they didn't give it away. Either that, or they were too emotionally involved in the argument with Luke.

I heard Luke pace a few steps towards where I was by the stairs and stop. "Why so you can lecture me about doing the right thing again? You're not my mother."

My heart leaped for Elizabeth. She had raised Luke like her own and I know how much it must have hurt her for him to say this. Even more, I felt sorry for Luke. Clearly this was his defense mechanism and losing his parents was not a wound that was closed.

"No, Luke. We won't lecture you anymore. You know exactly what you're doing and what you're capable of. We don't need to lecture you anymore for you to realize that you are good. We don't kill innocent people."

"We? What if that's who I am? You know what they say, the apple doesn't fall far from the tree! What if my father wasn't innocent? What if you have been cursed for eternity to save a guilty man?"

I heard Elizabeth gasp and Luke stormed past me up the stairs to his room. I stood frozen while I comprehended the words Luke just spoke. The whole reason they were Hunters was because of Luke's father. He had been accused of murder and was sentenced to be hanged in 1833. Christopher had made a deal with the Queen of Voodoo, Marie Laveau, to save Claude's life. In turn, they had vowed their eternal service to the underworld and thus began the curse. To say that Claude wasn't innocent, that he really did commit murder, was to say that Christopher cursed his family for generations and sentenced himself to immortality to save a guilty man. And Luke thought that he was the son of a murderer, and therefore evil himself. The Luke I knew was not evil, the Luke I knew had even believed in me and had helped save my life on more than one occasion. He had even saved the life of an innocent jogger. He laughed with me, comforted me. If he gave up hope in himself, where would his restraint be? Would he become like the Vasquez, who killed the innocent where they saw fit? I could never let him go there!

At that last thought I ran up the stairs after him. Christopher and Elizabeth might have said something to me but I didn't hear them; my face was twisted in thought and worry as I felt my way through the dark hall to Luke's room.

"What are you doing?" Luke asked while I was contemplating knocking. I pushed the door open guessing that was as good a welcome as any.

"I…I want to talk to you." I walked slowly into the warm room.

He scoffed, "Yeah, well, get in line."

He was sorting through a few things on his desk, and then went to the closet.

"I'm not going to tell you what you should or shouldn't do."

"Oh really?" He cocked one eyebrow at me from the closet.

I wrung my hands together. "Okay, maybe I lied. Maybe I will."

A smile crept on his face briefly before he turned back to his search.

I licked my lips not really sure where I was going with this. "I'm not really sure where I'm going with this." Honesty was best, I guessed.

He scoffed again from the closet.

"I know what you were trying to do down there. Do you hurt those that care about you to push them away?"

"Have I hurt you, Ana? Oh that's right- you don't care about me."

"Stop it, Luke. You know I care about you. I care about you a lot. I wouldn't be here if I didn't. You're not fooling anyone with that little charade you did downstairs. No one believes that."

Luke came out of the closet with a small box. "No one believes that? Really? I saw the look on Christopher's face before he could hide it."

I shook my head. "It doesn't matter what you are or who you were or what your father was. I know *you*, Luke. And I like you. I like all of who you are. I like how you make me laugh, I like how you show you care in ways that only you can do, I even like when you break the rules and sometimes even your bad attitude. The good, the bad, I like you."

Luke's head dropped and he exhaled as he paused his packing.

"But that you, whom I've come to know and like, is not evil. Could never be evil, no matter what you've done and no matter who your father might be. I don't care about all that, can't you get that through your thick skull?" I let out in a half-sob, half-laugh.

"Love."

"What?" I froze.

"You didn't say that you love me."

I felt my throat start to tighten. "I...What?"

"You said 'like.' What about 'love?' I need you to love me."

"Of course, we all love you Luke." *Why did my heart flutter?*

He brought his clenched fists to his side. "Dammit, you know that's not what I meant. Tell me that you're in love with me."

"Luke, stop."

"Tell me."

"I can't."

"You can't?" He mocked. "Then what the hell am I doing here? What the hell is the point in doing good, if I can't have you to spend the rest of my life with?"

"But—"

"Forget it, Ana. Just tell me, then, that there is no hope and I will leave you alone."

Silence was thick as I tried to drag a coherent thought from my brain.

"For someone who talks a lot, you're sure quiet now. All you have to do is tell me that there is no hope that we will ever be together and I will be out of your life. I'll stop trying to 'woo' you or whatever the hell you said I was doing."

"I can't," I breathed.

"You can't?" He asked with wrathful incredulity. "It's easy. If you can't even tell me there is no hope, then there must be a part of you that wants to be with me."

"Just stop it, Luke." I lowered my head in shame. Did my faults have to be exposed to everyone?

Luke came over to me and grabbed my arms, forcing me to look up at him. His beautiful hazel eyes pleaded with a passion I've never seen before. "I swear if you choose me, I won't kill anyone ever again. I won't go to the dance. I'll do whatever you want."

"Is that an ultimatum?" My voice rose and I came out of what seemed like a spell he had put on me. "The only reason you'll save my innocent uncle's life is if I'll be your girlfriend? *Never!* There's your answer."

He easily dropped his hands as I pushed them away. He held a lethally intimidating smile as he shook his head. "It's too late, Ana. You've given me hope. I will never stop trying. You will love me if it's the last thing I do." He picked up the bag on his bed and slung it over his shoulders. He leaned towards me as he headed for the door. "I'll see you at the ball." He gave my forehead a slow, sensuous kiss before I pulled away in disgust. Finally, my senses were working again.

"You're insane!"

I heard his laugh make its way down the stairs and I stood alone in his bedroom.

This was beyond repairable. Why hadn't I told him the truth? That I loved Hayden and there was no hope that I would ever be with him. Especially not now. His declaration that he would never kill another soul again if I loved him and his ultimatum that he would spare my uncle's life: that was so sinister. So evil. Shouldn't someone want to do good for the sake of doing good? I felt trapped. I was mentally kicking myself for not telling him right away that there was no hope but another part of me regretted not just agreeing to be with him to save Christian's life. Now, *I* was insane. I felt so guilty for even thinking that and didn't know how I could possibly face Hayden at this point. I managed to talk myself down enough to leave Luke's room. How could I think when I was surrounded by reminders of him? I sank into the darkened hallway wall and thought about what was wrong with me. Why was I twisted enough to consider taking Luke's ultimatum? The fact was, I couldn't be trusted with my emotions right now.

"I know what you're thinking."

I stopped in the hallway. "You do?" I sniffed and still couldn't bring myself to face Hayden.

"You can stop beating yourself up."

"Why shouldn't I be?"

Hayden sighed and I forced myself not to run to him and bury my face in his chest.

"It was wrong of Luke to use something you care about to try to get to you but it's even more wrong for you to beat yourself up over not considering it."

Of course everyone had heard our conversation. I groaned internally.

"I'm *not* regretting denying his offer. I can't believe he even said that." I told myself savagely.

"You care about your Uncle. It's only natural you would want to do anything to try to save him."

"Hayden, I..." I turned into him and he hushed me as he wrapped his arms around me. My heart ached and I wished my choices were simpler. Why couldn't I just love Hayden and that be enough? Why did I have to think of the future? Or the implications? Most of all, why did Hayden make it so easy to love when I made it so difficult. He had heard my entire conversation with Luke, my hesitance in denying him, and yet he saw me no differently. How could someone be so good and someone so evil? There were good people and there were evil people. I'd seen both in Luke. Was there a line, did those lines ever cross? How did you know which one was right? What were these feelings? What was love? Did I even know what that was anymore? Did I even know who I was anymore? I felt like locking myself in my room, indulging in my self-pity, but Hayden's hold on me tightened and a new wave a feelings came over me. I lifted my chin up and we walked downstairs to meet his parents.

Chapter Fifteen

❧

Throwing myself into school work was something I did to forget about things and the choices I would have to eventually face. I had planned to apply the same amount of enthusiasm when I got to work. I was slightly looking forward to the odd jobs and extra extremities that Zack would make me take. School was over and Luke was still nowhere to be seen. *Out of sight - out of mind,* I told myself. Or was it *not* out of mind? He certainly wasn't out of my mind.

"Have you seen him yet today?" I asked Hayden as we walked to the parking lot after school.

He shook his head, tight-lipped.

"You don't think he'll come to the ball on Saturday, then, right?"

His silence and the frown line that indented his brow told me what he was thinking.

I stopped walking. Why would Luke do this? To prove that I was wrong - that I couldn't change my dreams? Or to prove that he really was evil, that his father really was guilty, and that he was truly his father's son?

"Why would Luke do this?" I thought out loud. I didn't give him time to reply. "I wish I could figure out these stupid dreams. If I knew I couldn't change the future, then maybe I could work on accepting it." I knew I wouldn't. "But the fact that I don't know, it haunts me. And the thought of if I could but then I fail, well, that haunts me more. It just seems like everything is coming apart at once. I can't even—"

Hayden's soft lips came crashing down on mine and everything else seemed to float away. In that brief moment everything seemed right.

"What did you do that for?" We started walking again as I touched my fingers to my swollen lips.

"To distract you." He turned briefly with a slashing smile.

I smiled back dreamily. "Well, that worked." Hayden had spent the past twenty-four hours listening to my every thought and theory. I had even told him about my dream at the theatre, wondering if there was a connection there. It had seemed so long ago since I'd had that dream; trying to figure out what the dream meant and what Christine had wanted had taken the back burner to my current crisis. Despite Hayden's reassurances, he was right: I needed a distraction.

He slipped his hand in mine when we got in the car. He waited to back out, letting the line of other students leaving pass us. I saw Bailey from class waving as she walked by and waved back at her.

When I turned back to Hayden, I found him looking at me thoughtfully. "This may seem like a lot at the moment. But moments come and go. And pretty soon this will all be past you and you will have the answers that you're looking for. When that time comes, this will all seem insignificant and you will become stronger because of it. You already are."

"Why do you always know how to say just the right things? Are you ever less than perfect?"

He laughed satirically. "I am far from perfect, Ana. You should know that now. And the more you come to know about my nature, the more you'll see that. That's what I fear most."

I gripped his hand right back. "I'm sorry if I have given you any reason to doubt the way I feel about you. But that is never going to change. Never. Love is blind."

"Love is also arrogant and sometimes doesn't see its true ways. But this isn't about me. This isn't what I'm worried about. You're concerned with saving everyone's soul but at what cost to you? I think you should just take one thing at a time. Everything else will work out itself."

"Do you think that I'm not supposed to be seeing the future? That no one can really change the future, they can just try to mess with it and face the repercussions?"

"Honestly, Ana, I don't know. Everything I thought I knew changed the moment I met you. It opened my eyes to see that anything is possible."

"That's the hardest for me. Not knowing."

"It's okay to not have everything figured out. It took me a lifetime to learn about Hunters. I hope for your sake, it won't take that long to figure out who you are."

Was it really okay? Would it be okay to let what was going on with Marie slide? Would it be okay to just concentrate on stopping what was going to happen at the ball and not think about the consequences of trying to change the future? Did I even have that choice? I felt the need to have things figured out. I had to understand them but maybe I couldn't understand everything. Not just yet.

I caught a glance at the clock. "We'd better go. I don't want to be reamed out by Zack again."

"You're late."

"I know, I'm sorry but I came here straight from school." I stuffed my backpack in my dad's locker and peeled off my jacket just as quickly.

"I get off of school at the same time as you and you don't see me coming in late." Zack didn't look up from the sheet of paper he was reading over. "Oh, that's right. I don't sit and gossip with my friends after school. I actually need this job."

"I wasn't gossiping with my friends," I gasped, insulted.

"Your little boyfriend, then."

I laughed at the thought of anyone thinking Hayden was little.

"Yeah, that's what I thought. Suit up. You got boat inspections you owe me."

"I—," but Zack had left, leaving me alone to change in the locker room.

"Someone woke up on the wrong side of the bed," I mumbled.

"I heard that!" Zack yelled from the other side of the door.

"Good!" and I grabbed my things to change in the bathroom stall.

I had three boat inspections to do before I could leave and it would mean I would be staying a while. It wasn't as if I was in a hurry to go home. Hayden was taking his parents out tonight. *The master of distraction,* I thought, as it was clear Christopher and Elizabeth's moods were anything but cheery under the current circumstances. Something told me they weren't going out for a night on the town and I longed to tag along and know what Hunters did. This made me anxious and I quickened my pace in the water.

The sun was slowly setting as I entered the water to do my third and final dive. The orange ball in the sky reflected onto the water making the water look falsely warmer than it was. I would have to hurry before it got dark. Something about the Mississippi at night scared me. It was already hard enough to see through its muddy waters.

I ran out of air halfway through and had to resurface. I quickly took a new tank, not having the time to refill mine. *Just what I needed when I was trying to get done quickly,* I thought resentfully. When I was back underwater, I felt the day come to an end above me. My flashlight was my only light source. I suddenly felt chillier than the water around me. *Forget it, Zack, you'll have to finish this tomorrow.* I didn't want to stay in the water another minute. Everything felt wrong. I started my ascent to the surface when I felt a spine-tingling chill. I started to panic; emotions attached to the tingling came flooding back to me. Nausea took panic's place and I wished I didn't have a mouthpiece in at forty feet under water; in any other environment, I would have thrown up. I took a few deep breaths through the mouthpiece and convinced myself I was just scaring myself. I showed the flashlight all around me. Just to make sure. Nothing but darkness was beside me, which wasn't comforting in the very least. I started my ascent again, more anxious to get out of the water than ever. *It's not like my ears are ringing,* I told myself, remembering what happened the last time I felt the skin tingling and nausea. It was almost as if it were a signal that something, or someone, bad was coming. I continued to gradually kick my feet as I released air from my vest when I was halted. I wasn't moving. I felt like I was in a nightmare as I tried to kick my feet toward the surface again but wasn't moving. Only one leg moved. I was caught. Someone had my fin.

I was already panicking when my ears started to ring. I squeezed my eyes shut, trying to calm myself down. I must have just caught it on something. There would be no way someone was down there. I would have seen their light or their bubbles. But they wouldn't need light or bubbles if they weren't human. Suddenly, all the water around me felt claustrophobic. I was still a good thirty feet from the surface but it could have been inches or miles away. It was easy to die in water. Seconds trickled by as I tried to work myself free from what I told myself was an old fishing line. Still, I couldn't bring myself to shine the flashlight down by my feet. My hands shot to my ears as the ringing became suddenly painful. Something wrapped around my body, pulling the compressor from my mouth. My worst fears were confirmed. My leg was freed but the hold around my body suit was tighter. My lungs started to tighten with the breath I held and my heart beat wildly against my ribcage. I could not even scream at the thing that was trying to kill me. I was underwater and needed to save the air that was left in my lungs. I tried to shine the flashlight at my feet but saw nothing there. *That's because it's behind me.* I didn't have time to think about what *it* was or why it wanted me dead. I needed air. And fast. I could ascend without risking my lungs exploding from the pressure but I needed the thing to release me. I fought wildly against it and tried to reach my arms back to grab my emergency air compressor. A hold on my arms kept me from reaching around. Even more unsettling, the restraint didn't feel like human hands. My lungs tightened even more and I was going to have to release the breath or die. I tried to reach for my diving knife, hoping a weapon would work. Zack was supposed to be monitoring me; I held on as long as I could, hoping that he would notice something was wrong. I even foolishly thought Hayden would come to my rescue again. I struggled, feeling light-headed, trying in vain to reach my knife. I moved the flashlight, trying to see where I was grabbing when I felt something coming toward us. I didn't know whether I should feel relief or fear. Was it someone coming to save me or was it someone coming to help kill me? With a deep inhale through my mouthpiece, I prayed for the former. I aimed my light in its direction, not waiting another second to find out which one. No. Way. *Alligator?* I fought the monster behind me even harder and it suddenly let go. Shock momentarily came over me but I didn't have time to dwell; my lungs were dying. Two monsters were in the water around me. Two very different predators. I stole one more look at the alligator before unclipping myself from my vest and kicking with fury until I broke the surface of the water. I didn't stop swimming as I gulped in air. I quickly made my way over to the boat and flew up the ladder. I finally allowed myself to collapse on the boat deck when I knew I had made it safely out of the water. I kept sucking in breaths. I couldn't get enough air in my lungs. I felt the light-headedness return with a new symptom. And my eyes closed slowly around my consciousness.

I opened them again briefly when I felt the world drop beneath me. My eyes tried to adjust to the light as I saw the ceiling of the warehouse. I was inside and I was being carried. I fought to keep my eyes open, to see who had me, but no matter how hard I fought, the numbness of unconsciousness called to me and my eyes closed again.

I was forced to open them again when my chest was pushed with such force I thought my ribs were about to break. It was

Zack, his hair dripping droplets of water onto my face. He was giving me CPR, I realized. *I'm not dead, I just want to sleep.* I groaned and tried to turn away but he slapped my face. *Ow.*

"Stay with me!" I thought I heard him yell.

"Leave me alone, Zack," I groaned again. "You are always so mean to me," I babbled with as much coherence as I could manage. "You came to my house and won't even let me sleep. I'm not supposed to be working today."

"Come on. You have to get up. You can't fall asleep, now."

My surroundings came into focus and the warehouse was familiar. We were at Taylor Diving. I was working. I had been underwater, doing a boat inspection when…

I shot up as the memories came back. "Oh my god…"

"Shh," Zack hushed me, placing a hand on my shoulder. "Don't get up so quickly."

"Ow." My hands gripped my head at the sudden pain.

"Here, drink this." Zack handed me a cup of something hot. Drinking was the last thing I thought about doing but I took it from him anyway and took a sip of the coffee to help appease him.

"What the heck, Zack?" I winced at the pain from my own yelling. "You were supposed to be monitoring me. I almost died!"

"Don't you start with me. I was monitoring you. Why do you think you are here right now? How exactly did you almost die anyway?"

"I—I was caught on…something." I tried to think of another way of explaining just how exactly I almost died without sounding crazy by saying that there was something down there that grabbed me. "I am never, ever, going back in there again!"

"Just because you had one accident?"

"No. Because there are alligators."

"Alligators by the docks?" He sounded almost as nervous about the idea as I was. "You sure you didn't hit your head?"

Or not. I pushed him away from me as I tried to sit up but he stopped me. "You should just rest until there is enough oxygen back in your blood. You could have burst a lung ascending as fast as you did, ya know."

"If I didn't know any better I'd think you actually cared. Now let me up." I finally managed to break free of him and headed towards the locker room. "The only reason I didn't burst a lung is because I was so scared, I let out a scream the whole way up."

"It looks like your fear scared you," he winked at me.

I scowled back at him. "And how did you know how fast I surfaced, anyways?" I paused, my hand on the locker room door.

He shifted, running a hand through his hair. "You...you don't remember what happened?"

"Actually, I remember exactly what happened and I don't remember you anywhere near the water." My hands were on both hips as I regarded him skeptically.

"I think you hit your head, Ana."

I grunted as I turned on my heel and pushed the locker room door open.

It was late by the time I emerged from the warehouse. The cool winter air blew into my damp locks and I shivered. I inhaled deeply, offering gratitude to be alive. Again. Then panic sunk in. My head whipped around to the shell-covered parking lot outside our building. Hayden wasn't there. It was long past the time he usually picked me up. I wrapped my arms around my body, suddenly feeling very vulnerable and alone. After everything I just went through, I needed Hayden. I needed someone to talk to. Why wasn't he here, I wondered? And the hurt immediately went to concern. More importantly, if whatever was lurking at the bottom of the Mississippi was supernatural, why wasn't he called to Hunt? Why didn't he save me? It felt like such a childish thing to think. Hayden wouldn't always be there to save me, would he?

With the edges of my heart burning, I started walking across the parking lot.

"Do you need to go to the hospital?" I turned around to see Zack's back toward me, locking the front door.

"No," I said with more sadness than stubbornness.

He finished and turned toward me with a surprised expression. I waited for his sarcasm. When he didn't deliver it fast enough, I turned to continue walking. My footfalls were so angry a path of broken shells trailed behind me.

"C'mon, I'll give you a ride."

My body spun around to face him. "What, you ran out of snide comments?"

"Do you want a ride or not?"

I bit my lip as I considered my options. In the end, fatigue won over pride. I walked to his truck and got in without another word. "Thanks," I barely whispered as he turned the key to start the truck.

Zack wasn't trying to start a conversation on the drive back and although I wanted to ask him about the accident, I was relieved. I stared out the window, watching the blur of lights as we drove by. I was briefly aware of my phone vibrating in my backpack before my eyelids fluttered closed.

Chapter Sixteen

✣

"**A**na, wake up." His voice was soothing as it led me out of the fog of sleep. With a smile on my face, I stretched my arms out to wrap them around Hayden's neck. When he wasn't lying next to me, my eyes shot open.

"Oh my gosh." I looked around and realized I wasn't lying down, and I wasn't alone. I finally calmed down when the recent memories came back to me. "Oh."

"Sorry to disappoint. But you're home."

"How did you know where I lived?" I said, suddenly alarmed. Last time someone brought me home without directions, well...

"Uh, I have been here more than a few times with my pops?" He looked at me with suspicion and craze.

"What?" Desperation came out on my tone and he held my gaze until I looked at the house we were parked out in front of. It was my Dad's house. Of course he knew that. They didn't need to know I had moved out and I didn't see the need to tell them that tonight. I let out a weak laugh. "Right. Sorry, still waking up. Well, I'm going to go." I pulled the door handle and the car door flew open. I grabbed my backpack and stumbled out of his truck. I was not used to the height differences.

"Careful."

I listened for mockery in his voice but found it surprisingly absent. "Yep, I'm fine. Thanks for the ride, Zack."

"Anytime."

I looked at him, giving him one last chance to dare to make a comment about why he had to give me a ride home and why Hayden was a no-show. When he didn't, I said goodnight and shut the door.

I took baby steps up to the front door of my dad's house. Zack still hadn't left by the time I got to the front and I tensed, hoping he wouldn't want to see me go inside. I turned back, giving him a wave to signal he could go. He didn't. And I waved again until he finally got the picture, shook his head and left rather too abruptly. I let out a breath when he was finally gone. I realized I was just standing on the front steps like a stranger. I peeked through the sideline window. Inside looked warm and cozy. A perfect place to be on night like this. But this wasn't my home anymore. The sounds of laughter from inside confirmed that. I turned away, walking back the few blocks to where I lived now.

When I got close, I saw Hayden running out into the driveway, obviously hearing me approach. He scooped me into his arms and I was all too eager to fall into them.

After kissing me frantically, he spoke. "Where were you?" Then as if realizing something, he looked around the street suspiciously.

"Where was *I*? You were supposed to pick me up." The wind blew and I shivered again.

Hayden led me inside, not releasing my arm the entire time. When we got inside he turned to face me. "I'm so sorry, Ana. I got called," he paused, "and I didn't know if Luke would be there or how that would work out, so I had to go. Elizabeth said she would be happy to pick you up from work. When she got there, she said you were gone. It turned out to be nothing, so I came back home to see if you got a ride. My parents are still out looking for you." He finished frantically searching my face for any signs of injury before finally resting on my eyes. Then my lips. "If anything had happened to you..."

"Shh... I'm fine. But I need to tell you what happened."

I took a warm shower and then explained everything to Hayden as I was getting ready for bed. When I finally lay down for the night, I vaguely remembered Hayden saying he had to go out. I had no energy to form a protest. I had school in the morning and I knew Nikki would say something about getting beauty sleep. Whatever tried to kill me, Zack, Mr. Christian, Marie, Luke... all that could wait until the morning.

Chapter Seventeen

✤

I t was Friday, and finally the day before the ball. Tonight would be the celebratory 'night parade' and all the people running for court would be given one last opportunity to sway voters by being on Ecole's float. Since I was officially on the ballot, thanks to Nikki, that included me.

I woke up early, feeling more energized than I thought possible after the night before. I even went on a run around the neighborhood. I felt so alive afterwards; I could hardly remember that I had been so close to death in the first place. Hayden's parents were there when I woke but Hayden still wasn't back. We had a nice, yet quiet, breakfast together and I tried to cheer up Elizabeth by cooking with her. They gave me a ride to school and assured me Hayden would be back soon.

When I got to school, the atmosphere over was ecstatic, but I had a lot more on my mind than just the parade. Luke was gone and Hayden skipped school. Marie seemed like she was avoiding me and Nikki was everywhere, bouncing off the walls in her excitement. I felt alone and regretted telling Hayden about my diving accident last night. He would have been here with me instead of out searching for ghosts if I hadn't.

I dragged myself to my locker before first period to kill time. When I opened it, something fell out. My heart stopped as I, once again, automatically suspected the worst. I looked at the floor, and my mood instantly improved. Laying on the floor by my feet was a single rose whose petals looked blood-red against the shiny linoleum. I picked it up between my thumb and forefinger, removing with my other hand a scrolled note tied to the stem. My heart filled with warmth and spread to my smile as I unfurled the note. The handwriting showed it was not from whom I expected it to be from, but was familiar nonetheless.

You are safe with me. Meet me in the parking lot during lunch.

Love yours and forever,
Luke

Why did I still have a ridiculous smile on my face as I walked to English? Why didn't I leave the rose in my locker? Why did I keep rubbing the soft petals of the rose against my lip, inhaling the smell of flowers and the lingering scent of autumn? It didn't even bother me how foolish I looked as I sat in my usual desk in Mr. Atkins' class, my daydream only interrupted by someone calling my name.

"Hayden is so sweet. You're so lucky, Ana." Bailey was smiling at me in a similar day-dreaming state when I finally woke out of mine.

"Hayden?" I wondered why she had brought him up. *Did she know something?* I thought briefly before realizing the rose I still held in my hand. "Oh. Right. Yes, yes he is." I smiled at her reassuringly before Mr. Atkins started and she took her seat. Of course that was why she had brought him up. I was fondling a rose that wasn't even from my boyfriend. Why on earth would that make me feel so giddy? Because that was exactly what I needed. I felt alone today, and after last night, scared. To know he was watching and I would be safe had given me the same feelings deep in my stomach that I get with Hayden. Wasn't that one of the things I loved about Hayden? Did I even know what love was anymore? *What was wrong with me?*

As much as I wanted to listen to and distract myself with Mr. Atkins' lecture, I failed miserably. I even tried to get a head start on our final paper but couldn't get past the first sentence. I thought about Nikki and Marie, but didn't want to bore them with my problems. I didn't have the heart to spoil Nikki's good mood and Marie still seemed distant.

My heart leaped when Marie came to my side in the hallway during passing time. She nudged my shoulder and I smiled at her unspoken apology.

She examined my face and frowned. "What's wrong?"

I explained to her my near accident at work and she instantly pulled me into a hug. "I'm so sorry I was acting weird the other night. I just needed some alone time; you needed me and look how I acted."

"No, its fine Marie, you had a lot on your mind and I'm alive, aren't I?" *For now,* the somber thought flashed in my head.

"Yeah, but you don't look okay. Is there something else bothering you?"

"It's not a big deal, I'll be fine. Tell me what's going on with you and, well, you know," I tried to casually mention the voodoo. If she didn't want to talk about it, I was okay with that, too, but I needed her to know I was there for her.

"Don't you dare change the subject," she said with a smile and a gasp. I was glad my mention of the other night didn't turn her cold. "Tell me what's bothering you. You know I won't judge you."

"I...nothing, it's fine."

"Adriana Rae. I will not let you go to your next class until you tell me what's up."

I quickly clamped a hand over her mouth and drug her to the other end of the hall. "Shh! People are going to hear my middle name!" I stared at her, knowing that was her intent. "Fine," I spoke as I exhaled. She smiled satisfactorily. "I feel so stupid saying this, but, well, you know Luke, right?" Of course she knows Luke. Gosh, I am not good at this sharing thing. "Well, I know you guys haven't gotten the best impression of him, but you don't see the side of him that I do. The fact is, he has a good heart, and he's very sweet..."

"Oh my God, Ana!"

I hushed Marie before she could say anymore. "It's not like that at all. But I do care about him. And everything that's happened has just made my brain go in circles. I have felt more in the past few months then I have felt in my entire life. I guess I just don't know what to do with it all."

"I don't know what you want me to say..."

"Nothing. I don't want you to say anything. I'm sorry I even brought it up. I guess I just needed someone who would listen. Please, don't think badly about me. I love Hayden, I know that for sure. I just don't know if I love Luke as well."

"Wow, that's pretty serious, Ana. I have never, obviously, been in a situation like that. But I know that love is a powerful thing. It is also infinite. You can love another person without loving someone else less."

My thoughts spun over her words. "But if I did, what does that say about me? What kind of person does that make me?" Marie said nothing as I answered my own question.

If Hunters really only had one person they could love, only one person their entire lives were meant for, then either Hayden or Luke would live forever alone. But it wasn't fair to be doing what I was doing with Luke. I shouldn't have given him hope that we could ever possibly be together. I did care about him but if he couldn't see the difference between our friendship and something else, then we couldn't be friends at all. I had made my choice, and in the beginning he'd made his. It could never be different, couldn't he see that?

I got to my locker to put my books in before meeting Luke for lunch. When I opened it, I had yet another surprise inside. An oversized box now filled my locker. I pulled off the attached envelope and read the card. My heart fluttered again at the familiar penmanship.

Bring this with to lunch. You'll need it.

Love yours, always and forever,
Luke

The excitement to know what lay in the box pushed any thoughts of canceling the lunch with Luke completely aside. I pulled out the giant white box and slowly popped the top off. I set the box down, shaking out a plush velvet blanket that was as red as the rose. I shook my head in awe and wonder at what exactly he had planned for lunch. I clutched the soft blanket in my arms.

This is not a good idea I thought as I walked toward the parking lot in excitement.

Luke was standing outside his car waiting for me, just as I'd imagined. *I hope Nikki won't be too mad I'm skipping out on lunch with her* I thought as Luke opened the passenger door for me. As the car door shut with me in it, I kept telling myself to stop. But I couldn't. I was like the proverbial moth to a flame. My head said one thing and my body did the other.

Luke was smiling victoriously as he drove away from the school's parking lot. I hit his arm to knock off his annoying expression. That only made him smile further.

I looked in the back seat to see a neat wicker picnic basket and my heart stung. "So, what, a picnic? Oohh, how original," I tried to sound like I wasn't impressed.

Luke laughed at my attempt at sarcasm. "Yeah, something like that," he said around a laugh.

When we didn't stop after a while, I became skeptical. "Where are we going?"

"Just relax."

"Please don't tell me were going to Lafitte."

"God, no." He shook his head and I was glad he was as bothered by the memory as I was. "Just calm down. You'll see in about ten minutes."

I looked around and upon seeing we were in downtown, I started guessing again. "Are we going to get beignets?"

"Nope."

"Are we going to my bench?"

"No. Geez, Ana. You don't like surprises, do you?"

"I've just have had enough surprises in my seventeen years to last a lifetime."

"Well, this is a good surprise," he emphasized.

We parked in front of a meter around Jackson Square and I thought maybe Luke had lied about the beignet idea. I was getting out of the car when Luke came around to help me finish getting out.

"You don't have to do that, you know."

"I know," he said simply. I noted he had never held the door open for me before which reminded me of Hayden, who always had been the gentlemen. I frowned at the thought. "But I want to," Luke added, which made me frown even further. He handed me the blanket, then grabbed the picnic basket and my hand as he led me down Decatur Street. We passed the artists in front of the cathedral, pausing to laugh at a few caricatures.

"Samuel," Luke stopped at a carriage, nodding to a man who acknowledged him. "Mi'Lady," Luke joked as he held out his arm for me to enter the carriage.

I laughed. "You're kidding right?"

"No, not at all."

I shrugged, long past the point of return, and grabbed his arm to lift me into the horse-drawn carriage.

"You know you're not from the 1800s," I spoke when Luke sat down next to me.

"I know. But sometimes, all we have is our past."

"Then I guess I should say, 'thank you mi'lord.' Even though that's a different time period and location." People really needed to start brushing up on their history lessons.

"Whatever works." He winked at me and began to unfurl the blanket over me.

"Thank you." There was sadness to my voice as I realized the intimacy of said picnic.

Luke started pulling out containers of food as the carriage pulled away, the sound of hooves on concrete breaking our silence.

"So, what is this all for?"

"You're not very trusting of people are you? Can't you just believe that I love you and want to do something nice for you?"

"No," I said to all of his questions.

"Well, I wanted to bring you to the ball in a carriage. But since I'm not going to the ball, I guess we'll just do the carriage."

"What? What do you mean you're not going to the ball?"

"Geez, don't sound too excited about it, Ana. Have some restraint." He laughed sadly. "But yes, to answer you, you didn't want me to go to the dance, so I won't."

I impulsively wrapped my arms around him. The feel of his thumbs caressing my back made me peel away.

"It's not that I don't want you to go. I am just scared. About what might happen. You know that, right."

"It's fine. I don't care about a high school dance; I was just going for you, anyway. There is one important little detail you forgot in why this could never come true, though."

"What's that?"

"Why would your dad's friend be at our school's dance?"

I looked thoughtful for a moment. "Good point! Thank you so much. Thank you for all of this." I held my free hand out to show the carriage and picnic.

"It's nothing," he shook his head, looking away. "I didn't know what you liked so I just brought a bunch of stuff. I hope it's okay." We regarded each other in silence as we ate. I watched him quizzically as he ate, knowing he was just doing it for show. I frowned at the thought. "So, are you going to tell me what happened?"

I finished swallowing a bite of my vegetarian muffaletta. "Tell you what?"

"C'mon, Ana. When you were diving?"

"Oh." Now I remembered. "I actually had almost forgotten."

"I'm sure," he smiled darkly.

"What about it?" I asked, not understanding his concern or how he knew about it in the first place.

"You think I would leave you? I would never leave you, Ana. If I'm gone, it is to protect you. But I am always watching you from afar."

"Ok, stalker," I joked, but he wasn't kidding.

"Hayden had left you. His Hunts are more important to him than you. But I was there. I'll never leave you."

"Where were you when I almost drowned?" I bit my lip in anger at the mention of Hayden. How could he say that when he knew the consequences? But I didn't ask that. Instead I only wanted to know why he hadn't rescued me like I'd hoped someone would.

"I was there, I swear. I tried to get to you, I can't explain it but when I did you were already safe."

"Do you know what grabbed me?" I prepared myself for his answer.

"No. Not yet."

I nodded. Nothing was ever just black and white.

"What's with that guy you were with?"

"What?"

"Zack. I don't like him. You need to stay away from him."

"*Excuse me?*"

"I swear, Ana. Hayden is one thing. He can't die, but Zack... I don't think I could control my anger around him."

"You're completely insane, Luke! Stop the carriage." I called to the driver and threw the blanket off of me. "For one, Zack is a family friend. For two, it's not even like that. At all. For three— stop the carriage, please!" I yelled again as we were not yet stopping.

"You can't leave, yet. Please, Ana, sit down."

"Please let me off." I turned my attention back to Luke. "No, Luke. And for three, you are not my boyfriend and have no say in who I can and cannot be friends with."

"Ana…"

"No, Luke. This was a mistake. And thank you for making me realize that. Goodbye."

The carriage hadn't stopped completely as I hopped off. What was I doing? I had never been more indecisive in my life. I was so hot and cold. I was completely turned upside down by Luke and the only way to stop it was to avoid him for good. I didn't know where I would get the willpower to do so, but I knew if I kept this up, I would fail. Marie said that love was infinite but it didn't feel that way. It felt the more I opened up to Luke, the more I was pulling away from Hayden. Most of all, it felt wrong.

I knew what I had to do. I had to avoid Luke until I could figure out was going on with my emotions. The only good thing that came from this lunch was that I now knew Luke wouldn't be going to the dance. Now I just had to garner the strength to avoid him for another day-and-a-half.

Luke caught up to me as I made my way toward the cabs parked on St. Charles Ave. "Ana, stop. Go back to my car, now." He was trying to steer me by my elbow in the opposite direction.

"No, thanks. I'll just take a taxi back to school." I pulled my arm away as if he'd burned me.

"That is ridiculous, Ana, I will give you a ride." His voice rose as he spoke until he yelled the last part at me, causing a few nearby tourists to turn their heads.

Luke was distracted by the attention and I used that opportunity to jump in an awaiting cab.

"Just drive, I'm going to Metairie," my voice shook with haste as I spoke to the cab driver.

Sure, I could have saved twenty bucks and made Luke bring me back to school. But having some time away from him and giving my willpower a break was worth the expense.

I handed the cab driver, who didn't seem too happy about my destination, some cash and told him to keep the change.

The parking lot was full again with no students in sight, so I assumed lunch period was over. I looked at the time on my phone and it was already over fifteen minutes into my next class. Since I had my phone out anyway, I dialed Hayden's number. The wind blew a chill about the same time I heard Hayden's generic voicemail pick up. Where was he? I didn't think I ever remembered hearing Hayden's voicemail before. Suddenly, I felt very alone. It was the perfect moment to doubt myself because everything was starting to take a turn for the worse, it seemed. I thought I knew my friends but there was a part of Marie's life that was a mystery. I thought I knew Hayden but he never shared anything about Hunting with me and now, when I needed him most, he had disappeared. Most of all, I thought I knew myself but apparently I couldn't even trust that.

I walked back into school, heading straight to my locker, thinking I really didn't have anything better to do and I certainly not wanting to go home and mope.

I waited for Nikki outside her class. And she took one look at my face and said, "Oh no you don't."

"What?" I raised my shoulders, just as surprised as I was confused.

"I know that look."

"What look?" Was I that transparent?

"It's the look you give when you are trying to get out of something. I've seen that look right before you talked yourself out of going shopping with me and I am telling you right now Adriana, I am not letting you get out of doing this parade."

My mouth dropped open a little at how well she knew me. "What do you mean, doing this parade? I thought we were just taking our usual post on Canal Street?" There was definitely something she was not telling me...

"C'mon Ana, you know all the students running for royalty get to go on Ecole's float in the parade. You have to sway your voters!"

"Nikki!" I protested. I barely knew how I was going to make it watching the parade, let alone participating in it with everything that was going on.

She put a delicate fist to her mouth and cleared her throat, "Let me rephrase that. All students running for royalty are *required* to ride on the float."

"Nikki!" I nearly screeched.

"What?" She threw her hands up in the air. "You're the one who wanted to run for queen."

I shot her a look. "You're kidding, right?"

"You didn't seem to protest when Stephanie got in your business. Maybe it's because *someone* got all jealous about her hooking up with a certain bad boy?"

"Who told you that?" I groaned.

"Marie talks, girl."

The hall quieted and I knew the bell was about to ring. I sunk down right there in the hall and buried my hands in my knees. Nikki quietly sat down with me but didn't say anything.

I lifted my head. "And she didn't hook up with him."

"I know, honey," she patted me with pity. "How 'bout this: after school, Marie and I will come over to hang out and help you get prepared for the parade and then we can all drive there together?"

I must have really looked pathetic if she thought a makeover would cheer me up. But I nodded anyway, knowing I had to move forward. She stood up and held out her hand, offering to help me up. I took it and together we walked toward our classes.

I grudgingly left Nikki to go to my AP History class with Luke. When I walked in, classes had already started but Rachel hadn't started teaching. Everyone had turned their attention to me when I walked in, probably thinking it was supposed to be the teacher. Luke was in his usual spot, my empty desk next to his was painfully in the spotlight. A blush flushed my cheeks as I took the walk of shame to my desk. I succeeded in avoiding his gaze while I sat down.

"Hey." I pushed my lips together as I heard the velvety aloofness of his voice. Did he really think I didn't mean what I had told him earlier? Was he naïve or just hopeful? Even the prospect of finding out why Hayden was not back yet was not enough to bring me to speak to him. After my dream, his threat of killing Zack was just too real.

He sighed after I didn't reply. A small white paper bag was placed on my desk. "I thought you'd be hungry since you didn't finish our picnic."

My stomach growled treacherously and I opened the bag to find another sandwich and a clear plastic container of fresh cut strawberries, pineapple, and some other berries. I licked my lips out of instinct. He was right, I was hungry and that vegetarian muffuletta was delicious. Suddenly, I was not beneath eating what he had given me and I took out the sandwich. I ate quietly while I went over my notes from yesterday's class. Rachel still had yet to show, and the students started talking amongst themselves at the first chance they got.

"Is it good?"

Luke was still irritatingly trying to get my attention. I rose my eyebrows in indifference as I kept chewing, not taking my eyes off my notes.

"I'm sorry I got a little jealous..."

Jealous? He was downright possessive!

"I know I don't have a right to be, yet, but..."

My blood boiled when he said the word *yet* and I crinkled my sandwich wrapper loudly and stuffed it back in the bag. I licked the last of the olive salad off of my lips.

I was surprised to hear him let out a soft groan and from the corner of my eye I could see him shaking his head. "I love the way you eat."

I rolled my eyes.

"Where's your friend? She was supposed to start class eight minutes ago?"

"I know I was wondering the same th—" I stopped mid-sentence and turned back to my notes. It was as if he knew just what to say to get me to talk to him. And oh, how I did want to talk to him. Hayden still wasn't answering my calls or replying to the few texts I'd sent him. Nikki said that I didn't need to know where he was at all times and I should just give him his space. But Nikki also didn't know that he Hunted rogue supernatural creatures or that I had almost been killed, yesterday being roughly my third time. And Luke was there, like he always was, open and straight-forward with me about his motives. I closed my eyes at the intrud-ing thoughts. I didn't like where this was going and I resented the doubt that was building inside of me.

When I opened them, a new teacher had come into the room. He was a younger man with a pile of manila folders and papers in his arms. He dropped the load on Rachel's desk, adjusted his sweater-vest and then faced the class. "Hello, I'm Mr. Cary. Sorry about the wait, Ms. Vitale had an emergency and I will be your sub for to-day."

The general mood of the class uplifted at the mention of "sub." Everyone's except mine. And maybe Luke's. It was just too much of coincidence with the way she had been acting lately. With the way everyone had been acting lately. I managed to exchange a questionable glance with Luke and then half-heartedly listened to the substitute teacher's instructions for that day. I added Rachel to the list of things I had to figure out and started jotting down notes as furiously as he was writing them on the board.

I somberly walked out of the girls' locker room after my last class. Hayden was nowhere in sight. I checked my phone and still noth-ing. Now I was really starting to worry.

"Do you want to hear my theories?" Luke appeared at my side, causing me to misstep and nearly knocking me over into the line of guys leaving the boys' locker room.

I adjusted the strap of my bag slung over my shoulders. "No." I didn't know whether to be more worried or relieved that Luke didn't know where Hayden was, either.

"C'mon love, I'll tell you on the drive home."

I walked in the opposite direction, hoping to find Marie or Nikki. "No, thanks. My friends are coming over after school so I'll just get a ride with them."

Of course I didn't get off that easily and Luke walked beside me back into the school. "I'm guessing from your demeanor that Hayden hasn't called you since he left early this morning?"

I scoffed. I wondered if Luke would ever get tired of the one-sided conversations.

"Which must mean that he must be with Tatiana who came in town last night."

Now Luke was making up girls to turn me against Hayden? He was really starting to irritate me but that was what he wanted, wasn't it? To get a rise out of me? "Never heard of her," I said indifferently.

Luke mocked being appalled. "You mean Hayden never told you about the Russian princess who's madly in love with him?"

I stopped walking and my hands balled into fists. "You're lying."

"Me? Lie?" He leaned toward my ear as he 'tsked me. "You know I have never lied to you." And I was pretty sure he hadn't. Either way, he must have known this piece of timely information would feed right into the part of me that was completely impulsive and irrational. "Why don't you call him and ask him yourself?" I turned to face him. Darkened hazel eyes looked up at me through lowered brows. "Oh, that's right, he's not answering is he?" *because he's hiding something* laced his last words.

"I hate you," I whispered spitefully.

He gave me that cocky, one-sided smile that probably brought men and women alike to their knees. "Well, you know what they say, love and hate both stem from the same place."

I tried to think of a smart reply to that but I came up with nothing. I just kept thinking about the first time Luke revealed his true feelings for me on the beach in Tampa. I think my exact words were, *"...but I thought you hated me?"* and then he told me he loved me. And then he kissed me. And I kissed him back.

"Rrg!" I grunted my frustration and left him standing alone in the hallway with that stupid smile on his face. "You're delusional!" I said over my shoulder as I made my way to Nikki's locker.

"See you at home, love!" Luke said with amusement in his voice, loud enough for everyone to hear.

Chapter Eighteen

❦

"Thanks for the ride, Marie," I said as I threw my book bag on the bed in my room.

"No problem, we were coming over anyway." *What happened to Hayden?*, were her unspoken words.

"So, I knew you wouldn't have a whole lot to go off of, so I brought some cute Ecole T-shirts; do you have some blue leggings, those would be *perfect*?" Nikki's voice faded as she entered my closet to help me pick clothes to wear for my appearance on the float. Attire would be 'anything goes' as long as it was in the school spirit. Masks were required and I wondered what she had in mind for that.

"Check the built-in drawers on the left," I told her, still unsure of the extent of my own wardrobe. Hayden had my room and bathroom stocked with everything I never had. As much as I was grateful, I was overwhelmed. Nikki, with her passion for clothes and candy, helped me put it to good use.

As Nikki raided my closet and Marie my books, I was thinking about how I would get through tonight without Hayden. I had hoped he would at least call me by the time the parade started.

But all I was doing was hoping. Hoping he would be home. Hoping he'd call. Hoping he'd still love me. What was that about? Surely, people in normal relationships didn't think those sorts of things. Then again, nothing about my relationship with Hayden was normal. How was it that I was able to manage life without him just fine six months ago? Very dully, but fine. Now it was if he had become so entwined in my life that I couldn't think without him. He had truly come to possess me. As much I told myself I was just worried about his safety, there was that insecure part of me that said he had left me, that he had just changed his mind and left me. It concerned me most of all because this was a time when I was questioning my love for someone else, and it didn't help that I was also questioning his love for me.

"Hello, space case?" Nikki took the cherry sucker out of her mouth with a plop. "What are you thinking about?"

"Hm, I wonder what?" Marie had found a book that piqued her interest and sprawled out on my bed to read. There was humor in her voice and I was glad to hear that things were almost back to normal between us after the night we opened her voodoo chest. "Or whom?" She let out a girlish giggle that was completely unlike her.

Her mood made me feel playful, and I picked up the nearest thing, a tube of mascara, and chucked it at her.

"Hey," she squealed and snapped the book shut.

I smiled and turned back around on the stool of my vanity. I looked at Nikki through the mirror as she emerged from my closet, saying, "I was trying to get your opinion on an outfit before you spaced out on me. Now you will just have to try all of them on." She threw a sizeable load of clothes on my bed and I groaned quietly. She came up to me at the vanity, beaming at my supply of products. "I get to do the makeup, Marie you can do something with," she fluffed my hair, "all of this."

"Hey," I protested at her playful insult.

Marie sat up from my bed and came to join us at the vanity. We looked at each other in the mirror for a while before Nikki said, "Let's get to work!"

When I finally was free from the grasps of my well-intentioned friends, I looked at my phone.

6:32PM. No missed calls. No new texts messages.

I wondered how I would be able to bring my cell phone with to the parade. I couldn't bring a purse and with the outfit Nikki had picked out for me, there was not an inch of clothing that wasn't clinging to my skin. I gave one last longing look to my phone before leaving it on the charger by my bed.

As I walked down the curving staircase, I heard Nikki's laughter mixing with Luke's seductive voice. *Great*, what now?

"What's a great idea?" I asked, jumping in on their conversation.

Luke turned toward me with a wicked smile that could only mean he was up to something.

"Luke's going to give us a ride to the parade," Nikki spoke for him, totally buying into his plot.

"Well, I was going anyway so I thought it would make sense if we all just rode together." I totally saw past Luke's feigned innocence at this coincidence. He was motivated, and now I knew he was calculating as well.

I looked at Marie to see if she had bought in as easily as Nikki had. She shrugged. "It would save me gas." Her face was apologetic.

My teeth sunk into my lower lip as I gave Luke a deadpan expression. I could drive myself, but I didn't think they would let that fly. Nikki had already deemed me a flight risk. And it wasn't like I would be spending time with Luke; we wouldn't even be alone. I had to be on the float 45 minutes before the parade started so they would have to drop me off at the warehouse, anyway. I guess it would be okay for Luke to look after them while I was in the parade...

"Fine," I conceded.

Luke gave me a victorious, closed-mouth smile and held out his hand to lead us toward the garage.

Nikki continued her conversation with Marie as they started toward the garage. As I went to follow them, Luke stopped me. I stared at his hand curled around my arm, acutely aware of his touch.

When I looked up at him, his eyes became stormy. He licked his lips and then bent down to whisper in my ear. The heat of his breath tickled the sensitive area of my neck as he whispered, " You can't expect me to play nice when you wear something like that. I'm afraid I simply won't be able to keep my hands off of you."

My jaw dropped open. His words appalled me—and at the same time excited me.

I recovered my composure. "You'd better keep your hands off me, unless you want me to break your fingers." I gave him my best menacing smile. Where was this side of me coming from? Strangely, I knew.

"Ohh," his chest rumbled with laughter. "Is that a threat or a promise?"

"Both," I snapped as he slowly made his way around to my other ear. This had to stop.

"I look forward to any time where you touch me." He had circled me, like he was a vulture and I was his prey.

"You're disgusting!"

"We'll talk more of what I am later, love. Right now, your friends are waiting." At his last words, he left me there in the hallway, weak-kneed and boiling with anger.

"No, we will not talk about this later!" I called after him, but it was too late, I had already heard the door to the garage open. And he'd had the last word.

I uttered a minced oath, blew a curl out of my face and stubbornly followed him out.

Five minutes later, I was in the garage standing outside Luke's truck. Luke had started the truck, and Nikki and Marie were already in the backseat. There was no way I was going to sit next to him, regardless of his plans. A thought occurred to me and I opened the back door to meet their confused faces. I smirked and squished myself in.

"There's no way I'm sitting up here alone like I'm some damned driver," Luke protested, looking irritated that his plan had backfired on him.

I tried to contain my laughter. "The car doesn't drive itself. And if you're not up for the job, we'd be happy to drive ourselves."

"You know that's not what I meant." He gave me a long look in the rearview mirror. "You know I'll take what I can get, Ana." And he pulled the gear into drive.

I was acutely aware of Luke's gaze on me the entire ride. I squirmed in my seat at the reflection of his intense hazel eyes and tried to pay attention to the story Nikki was telling us.

I caught the tail end of her sentence when I suddenly wished I had heard the whole thing. "She won't mind that you are going with us?" Nikki had asked Luke.

"Wait, what?" I gripped the seat in front of me. "Who won't mind?"

"Hello—Stephanie? Luke was supposed to be going to the parade with her. For her." Nikki looked up thoughtfully. "I'm not really sure how that works since she is going to be on the float with you."

"*What?*" I was stunned with both pieces of new information. I didn't know why I hadn't thought of it before. Of course Stephanie would be on the Ecole float since she was also running for Queen. But Luke on the other hand… I thought he had ended it with her. I didn't know why, but lately I was more repelled by her than before. I really meant it when I told Luke 'anyone but her.' I didn't trust her one bit. Something about her, besides her usual cruelness, just rubbed me the wrong way.

We pulled up to the warehouse where the floats were stored before the parade. I was a little disappointed that we had arrived already and I wouldn't be able to finish the conversation.

"Oh my God, we're here. Good luck, Ana!" Marie reached over and squeezed my arm. I was glad someone was nervous for me.

"Nah, who needs good luck? She looks great if I do say so myself!" Nikki was proud of her makeup job. I was really impressed as well. It was like she was an artist and my face was her canvas. Instead of a mask, Nikki had painted one on my face. It was subtle but the butterfly wings made my eyes look exotic. I could hardly believe it was my reflection staring back when I had first looked at myself in the mirror.

"Thank y'all so much, I really appreciate it." I gave my friends meaningful glances before opening the door. "Luke, may I have a word please."

"Of course," he smiled smugly.

I came around to his side of the vehicle and led him a few steps away from the truck—and Nikki and Marie's earshot—before I started with my inquisition.

"What's up with you going with Stephanie?" My hands automatically went to my hips and his gaze followed me there so I crossed my arms instead.

He shrugged like he didn't have a care in the world, and why would you if you were Luke Boudreaux, gorgeous, rich, and immortal? I swallowed. "Well?"

"That was before all of this."

"All of what?" I realized I wasn't trying hard enough to ignore him, that I was actually leading him on. And that realization struck me like a splash of cold water. It felt awful.

He must have seen something on my face because then he replied, "Stop worrying about if it's right or wrong. You can't change how you feel."

"You have no idea how I feel." He was right, I couldn't change how I felt, but I sure as hell could change how I acted on it.

"Admit it, you are jealous."

"I am not jealous!"

"Look at you, Ana. Your cheeks are a delicious shade of pink and you're all flustered. You look so cute when you get upset."

"You're insane!"

"You didn't even get like this when I told you about Tatiana and Hayden."

My breath hitched and I struggled to find the right words. "Because I trust Hayden!" I blurted out.

"Oh, Ana," he smiled, still looking irritatingly calm as he stepped forward and caressed my cheek with the back of his hand, "you try so hard to keep away from me. Yet, the very fact that you can't is what keeps me going. It's what gives me hope."

I clenched my teeth together. "Well, your *'hope'* is walking away."

And I turned and left him there without another word because that was what I had to do. If I was, as he said, incriminating myself the more I struggled with him, then I just had to not say anything at all. I was so flustered as I walked into the warehouse that I didn't take notice that someone had been watching from behind a float.

Chapter Nineteen

✤

When I entered the warehouse, I was overwhelmed with the display of colors and the colossal floats. I had never seen a float so close up and it was my love for New Orleans and memories of Mardi Gras that made me feel giddy at the prospect of riding on one.

Mardi Gras. The greatest free show on earth.

Krewes are carnival organizations that put on the parades. New Orleans has a ton of different krewes and they all have different parades, royalty, and throws. The Krewe of Hermes was famous for their night-time parades and each year had a different theme. The composition was a highly-kept secret and they did not reveal the theme until the day of the parade. One of the first floats I saw was decorated like a meadow with cat tails, complete with colorful flowers and butterflies. A banner over the top said "Visions of Valhalla." *The theme of the parade.* I smiled. I took a minute to admire the other floats in the building. It was interesting to see all the behind-the-scenes work and how detailed it was. My favorite float was also the most elaborate one, with a model of a woman Viking warrior on the front. The entire float was lit up with neon lights and I knew it would be the brightest float on the streets that night. High on the float, already settled in his chair, was the king who was outfitted regally, everything from his crown to his gloves. His mask covered his entire face, purposely disguising his identity. Krewes and their royalty inspired such intrigue, such mystery. The king's face was angled toward me as I walked by and I gave him a curt nod, not sure if he was looking at me or not.

A lot of people had already arrived when I got there and even with Nikki's amazing make up job, I was starting to feel underdressed. I couldn't imagine what some of the costumes must have set people back.

After roaming for a bit, I found the Ecole float. Ecole was lucky to have its own float in the parade. Usually the floats were the krewes own and most of the schools only were able to participate with marching bands and banners. Nikki had informed me it was because the principal was a member. All I knew was that we had the best Mardi Gras celebrations because of it.

Our group was comprised of five girls and three boys, a few teachers, administrative personnel and chaperones. I didn't see Stephanie yet, so I assumed it would be six girls. Some of the girls turned and looked at me as I approached. I gave them a tight smile. I awkwardly went to stand next to them when a chaperone with a clipboard approached.

"What's your name, hon'?"

"Adriana Alexander."

She tapped her pen and smiled. "Ah. I was glad to see that you entered a late application."

"Thank you," I smiled and didn't correct her that it was actually Nikki who entered for me.

"You'll be front left, between Stephanie and Josh."

"Thank you," I repeated. I paled as she walked away toward the next student.

Just perfect. Well, at least *I* was on time, I thought proudly.

We waited there for a while as last-minute preparations were made to the float. The girls had ignored the requirement for attire that was in school-spirit and were in everything from Venetian-style dresses to tutus and boas in purple, green and gold. The boys were all friends, and had obviously coordinated their outfits; they were dressed in matching blue suits with bowler hats and shimmering gold masks. I felt silly standing there quietly while everyone was talking to each other until a girl I recognized from Trig complimented my outfit and started a conversation about upcoming assignments.

We were more than ready by the time the float was ready to be loaded. The chaperones reminded us of the rules and what we'd be doing, and gave us each a box of goodies to throw out to the crowds.

"I'm here!" Stephanie sung out as we were getting onto the float. She had really outdone herself. She was dressed in an Ecole-blue sequined ball gown with a matching blue feathered half-mask. It wouldn't have been unusual, if it weren't for the array of peacock feathers encircling behind her. She also had forgone any Mardi Gras beads around her neck, probably figuring they took away from the elegance of the dress.

"Oh, there you are Stephanie." The same chaperone that helped me walked over to her. "We thought you were a no-show."

"As if I would miss the parade!" She put her manicured hands on her hips in true Hollywood starlet style. I gave her no more than a glance and concentrated on the float.

"All right, everybody on. It's Showtime!" The chaperone shooed us onto the float. The boys were high-fiving and the girls were giggling in excitement. I smiled at Lacey-from-Trig and then my smile died as I took my position next to Stephanie. I wished I'd known Josh better so I could have at least imagined I wasn't sitting next to Stephanie. But as the float started to move, I realized it wouldn't matter; Stephanie knew Josh. She spent most of the ride to St. Charles, the start of the parade, talking to him over me. She did a good job pretending I wasn't even there. *But I swear, if a peacock feather hits me in the face one more time...*

"Throw me something, mister!" A young boy called out, instantly changing my mood as I recognized the famous slogan. I smiled as I threw some Ecole-colored beads and small foam footballs donning our Trojan mascot out to the awaiting crowds.Night-time parades were fun because of the lights used on the floats. I had only missed the Krewe of Hermes parade once in my life, and never missed the Rex parade, because their krewe had the best throws. Even when my dad was traveling, he never missed carnival season.

I was quick to forget who was standing next to me as everyone else instantly had an attitude of camaraderie. I couldn't remember the last time I'd spent so much time laughing and smiling. The crowd was as interesting to look at as the floats; they sometimes even had better costumes. By the time the float made its way back to the warehouse, my cheeks were sore. I was surprised by how quickly the time had flown by. The crowds had been the largest I'd seen yet, and my heart swelled at the perseverance of New Orleanians. Even though the parade was over, there was no doubt that everyone would still be dancing until dawn. Katrina was not that many months behind us, but it was clear: New Orleans was back.

❧

Luke and Marie were waiting for me outside the warehouse when we finished cleaning up.

"Ana, you looked awesome up there!" Marie hugged me as I approached Luke's truck. "Nikki left with her 'rents, but *she bids you farewell.*"

"Ah, and I was so looking forward to her gushing." My tone was a bit sarcastic but it was true, I was looking forward to her commentary. "I was trying to look for y'all around Lee's Circle but I guess you were on the other side."

"No, we definitely saw you." Luke was standing by the hood and I hated that he held an expression of admiration and pride. I sighed when I realized I still hadn't heard from Hayden. I had hoped that he would surprise me and just appear as I was floating down Canal Street. It hurt that he hadn't been there.

A chill ran through me and I rubbed my bare arms with my hands. "Oh, no. I must have left my shawl on the float! I'll be right back."

Luke threw his arm around my shoulder, "Leave it, we'll get you another one. We have some celebrating to do."

"I can't, it's Nikki's and she would kill me if I lost it. Start the car, I'll just be a minute." I took off into the warehouse, hoping someone would still be there to let me in. The door was unlocked and the overhead lights were still on, so I figured there must still be people working on their floats. I made my way to where the back of the building where the Ecole float was parked.

I found Nikki's sweater just where I had left it on the float. I grabbed it and went to run back to the truck when the lights flickered once, twice, and then went out. My heart sped but I still didn't rule out any reasonable explanations. "Hello?" Everyone had probably just left for the night and didn't realize I had come back in. Or maybe the lights were on a timer? "Hello?" Maybe they were motion- censored? I took a few steps in almost complete darkness. I heard footsteps and that's when I started running towards the exit. I heard the power click and a single light above me turned on. I stopped running and looked all around me.

"Adriana," I turned at the familiar sinister voice. Stephanie had appeared in front of me, a frightening gleam in her eyes.

"What do you want, Stephanie?"

I thought I had managed to get through the parade with no snide comments but apparently I would not be that fortunate tonight.

"You will not be Queen." Her face burned with anger and it was then that I noticed that her peacock tail was missing, her hair mussed and dress torn.

I took a step back as she approached me. "It's just a stupid school dance, calm down."

She laughed darkly as if she didn't hear me. "You can't be Queen, if you're finally dead!" She grabbed my arm in one quick motion.

...*if you're dead.* I didn't register the *finally* part. I just knew that with any mention of the word dead, I needed to get out of there fast. I tried to yank my arm free but she was surprisingly strong. It was the feeling of being trapped that caused me to panic. "Let me go, Stephanie." When she didn't, I kicked her as hard as I could with my free leg. She keeled over long enough to let my arm slip free, and I screamed as I ran away, knowing Luke would be able to hear me.

Something about Stephanie was not human as she instantly caught up behind me, sending me falling to the floor with one powerful push. I turned over to find Stephanie hovering over me before she pinned me down with her arms and legs.

Her manicured nails felt painfully sharper then they looked as they dug into my neck. "I am going to enjoy ripping your head off from your body. You won't look so appealing then."

"You're crazy!" I spit at her.

"Let her go!" The sound of Marie's voice frightened me. Why hadn't Luke made her stay in the truck?

"Marie, you need to get out of here!" I yelled at her through strained breaths.

"Follow your friend's advice, witch, or I'll have to shred you to pieces as well."

I was taken aback by the sound of a new voice. It was deep and sounded like many voices on top of each other. That voice, though, was coming from Stephanie, and she was talking to Marie.

"Wrong being," I heard Marie say when I felt Stephanie's body ripped off mine and watched as she flew to the other side of the room. I got up to see Stephanie's body crumbled on the ground below a float. Shreds of paper mache and purple, green and gold glitter were floating down to the ground.

"What *are* you?" Luke was by my side, helping me to a stand, but he was talking to Marie, whose hands were still held out defensively. I quickly put the facts together, and realized just exactly what Marie was.

"Never mind that. Focus on her!" Marie pointed to Stephanie who was already trying to stand again. It was shocking to see Stephanie recover from that, especially after seeing the hole she left in the float.

"How is that possible?" I wondered out loud.

Luke sniffed the air. "Sulfur." He growled, looking completely feral.

I watched Luke, concerned at his drastic change in behavior until Marie said, "Demon." Then I realized Luke was in Hunt mode.

Stephanie/Demon smiled, completely unaffected by the blow, and we all stood there defensively waiting for its next move.

The Neptune float next to us started to shake and before I could react, I was whisked away to the other side of the building. Luke set Marie and I down in time to see the float crash to the ground right where we had been standing.

Luke cursed, and I realized he wasn't going after it because that would leave us vulnerable.

"Don't have all your powers in your current form," Luke taunted. "Why don't you come out so we can play hardball?"

I didn't know what powers the demon was limited to in Stephanie's body, but I knew what Luke was doing. As long as the Demon was in her body, in order to kill it, he would have to kill her, too.

"So you can save the human? I'm not stupid. I won't give up my only protection." The voice that came from Stephanie was still strained and deep.

Luke shrugged. "I could care less if a human dies in the cross fire. Ah well, I guess this Hunt won't be much of a challenge after all."

I looked at Luke to see if he was bluffing but he gave nothing away. What scared me was that I didn't think he was.

Another object came flying at us and I found myself, once again, moved in a blur. I steadied myself as Luke put me down and shoved me behind him.

"Don't. Touch. Her."

I looked around, but Marie wasn't next to me. I found her at the same spot we'd left her, the head of the Neptune float burning in flames beside her. Marie's hands were still held out toward the float and she was shaking.

The Demon remained where it was, laughing. "Protective of her, are you? Thank you for revealing that. It will make it so much more fun when I tear her to pieces."

Luke growled again as he ripped a pole from a float with his bare hands. "It will take me 1.5 seconds to impale this through your heart. The iron will kill your demon form."

"And the humans...?"

Luke shrugged again. "We've already established this: I just don't give a damn."

The demon let out a sole laugh. "You are alone, with two, well, one-" he looked at Marie, "and-a-half, humans to protect. Do you really think in those 1.5 seconds that I couldn't have that light overhead crush her? Or that float? Or pole? Or truck? There are so many ways to die in here. And the only way she's remaining alive right now is because she's relying on your—"

A blur shot by my face, ramming straight into the demon and taking it down. I looked beside me to discover it wasn't Luke. If Luke was surprised by our new visitor, he didn't show it.

A woman was holding the demon down and it thrashed beneath her. I felt someone's hand touch my shoulder and I looked to my right, startled. "Hayden," my relief came out in a sob.

I threw my arms around him and buried my face in his neck. We pulled apart when the woman called out to us.

"Marie, are you all right?" I ignored the woman, running toward Marie and mentally assessing her for any wounds.

"I...I'm fine." She stared at her hands as they shook. I grabbed one of them in mine as the woman restraining the demon called out for Marie this time.

"I recognize that voice," I spoke as we anxiously walked together toward the demon. When we stopped, the woman threw back her chestnut hair and I saw exactly who it was. Rachel Vitale.

Chapter Twenty

❖

I was speechless as Rachel focused on Marie. "Cast a spell to free her body or I will have to destroy her."

"I…I can't," Marie said in a shaky voice. "I don't know how. I don't even know how I did what I did."

"Let your emotions guide you. The rest is ingrained in your blood," Rachel coached.

Marie thought for a moment, inhaled a deep breath but then shook her head in defeat.

Rachel shrugged. "Very well," she said, and gripped the sides of Stephanie's head.

"Wait!" Marie called out to stop her. "I will try." Marie got down on her knees next to Stephanie, or whatever it was that was inside her, who was still thrashing about, trying to get free.

Marie held her hands out in front of her and squeezed her eyes shut. When nothing happened, she opened them with a disappointed exhale.

"Try again," Rachel barked.

Marie looked at her and then went back to trying to rid Stephanie's body of the demon.

"Think about what this monster could do to humans if un-leashed on New Orleans. Go back to what you felt when it was on Adriana, about to kill her."

I gasped as a dark smoke started to come from Stephanie's body. It swirled around her until it covered her like a blanket.

"That's it," Rachel encouraged, and let go of Stephanie to take a step back.

Marie swallowed and squeezed her eyes shut tighter. Stephanie's body rose from the ground as the dark smoke strug-gled to keep inside of it. I heard Marie call out in anguish, as if the task were just as difficult for her. "C'mon Marie," I whispered in worry.

Marie let out one last scream before the black smoked disap-peared as if it had been suctioned out, and Stephanie's body, now limp, fell back to the ground. There was a collective sigh, and Marie fell back, exhausted.

I ran over to her and helped her to a stand. "Are you okay?"

"I...I'm fine. Just tired," she lied.

"Do you want to talk about it?" I asked, hoping she would. When she didn't answer, I corrected my sentence. "I'll be here when you're ready to talk about it."

Rachel barked an order, "Luke, take Stephanie home. She should be out of it for at least a day. Tell her parents she had too much to drink."

Luke nodded. "Won't she say something when she wakes up?" I studied his expression, wondering if he meant we should just get "rid" of her. The thought of him still being so cold and calculating sent me reeling back.

Rachel shook her head. "She won't remember anything that happened after the demon took possession of her body, which, I am guessing, happened right before the parade. These types of spirits can only last a few hours inside a human before they have to feed on it and find a new host." She spoke so informatively and coolly. I had known for a while that she knew more than she let on. I just didn't know how much. And I never would have guessed she would be one of *them*.

I swallowed at the picture Rachel had painted in my head. Essentially, Marie had saved Stephanie.

"Thank you, Marie." I turned toward her to find her looking ill.

"Take Marie home, first. She needs to rest," Rachel added to Luke's duties.

Marie and I nodded at each other as we walked away with Luke, who was carrying a still-limp Stephanie.

I sadly watched them walk away. I felt horrible that people were getting hurt because of me. Hadn't I caused enough trouble with Hayden and Luke? Now Rachel, Stephanie and Marie were involved.

I felt a strong hand rest on the small of my back and turned to Hayden with a sigh, "Hayden." I burrowed my face in his chest as he held me. The scent of him made it feel like I was home again.

"I know," he said, reading my thoughts.

I pulled back from him. "Where were you? I tried calling and leaving messages. You worried me so much."

"That was my fault." Rachel came towards us; her demeanor had seemed to change since this whole incident. She was no longer the meek, kind teacher I knew. She was stronger, more intimidating, and more informal. "Hayden was tracking me, and I must say, I gave him a run for his money."

I shook my head, not understanding. "Why? What are you?" I remembered that she hadn't been in class today and we'd had a substitute. Hayden was also missing during that time, so the facts checked out.

She tilted her head with a warm smile, a smile that did not suggest she'd just helped kill a demon. A smile that was almost…

"I'm your mother."

…motherly.

Chapter Twenty One

✤

My eyes wouldn't stop blinking. I looked at Hayden for confirmation. He nodded triumphantly with a hesitant smile. Hayden knew about my mother—or lack thereof. He was the only person to whom I'd admitted trying to find her. He knew how I felt about her and my lingering questions. Yet he still looked at me, waiting to gauge my reaction.

My *mother*?

He'd found my mother?

I *had* a mother?

Then, the biggest realization came to me. *Rachel* was my mother. I had known Rachel for almost two years. She was my teacher, she was my friend. We'd talked and emailed each other. I shared things with her that I couldn't with Nikki or Marie. And she was my mother!

"*You're* my mother?" The words came out with disbelief and thinly concealed wrath.

"Adriana..." She used my full name to scold me. Like a mother would. Had she expected me to be happy? To welcome her with open arms?

Yes, of course there was a part of me that was excited, that couldn't wait to pick up things where we'd left off. To make up for time lost. But that was a naïve, childish fantasy. The fact was, she had known me for two years and had never said anything. She had listened as I complained about the situation with my father. And my father! He had to have known she was my teacher, and he didn't say anything?

I gripped the sides of my head with my hands. "Oh my gosh."

"Ana," Hayden wrapped his arms around me, but I pulled away.

I looked at him apologetically. It wasn't his fault. He was trying only to find out what I was, how could he have known it would lead to this? "Hayden, please just bring me home."

"Adriana, I know you must have a lot of questions." Rachel held up her arms to stop us.

"Heck yeah, I do!"

"I will explain everything in time."

I snorted. Of course, it wouldn't be that easy. No one could ever just tell you everything! Everyone had to be so dang cryptic! My chest heaved with rising anger. "Hayden, please."

He nodded and led me out of the warehouse. I heard Rachel click her tongue as if she was about to say something else but she didn't.

When we were in the luxurious confines of Hayden's familiar black sports car, he started to speak. "Ana, I'm sorry I didn't tell you what I was doing."

"It's okay. You couldn't have known."

"When I first saw you again tonight, there was this look on your face. It was one of relief but with something else."

I let out a puff of breath. "I thought you weren't coming back."

"Adriana... you can't be serious."

"I don't know what was going through my head." I lacked any emotion to my words. I was drained of everything: surprise, anger, fear, love.

"Since the dive accident, I had been trailing the being that had come after you, when I noticed other beings were there as well. One of those was another of my kind. That's when I started tracking your mother. I lost track of time and I never imagined that you would take my absence like this. I assumed you trusted me."

"I do."

He turned my chin to face him, and his gaze raked my body hungrily before pressing a punishing kiss to my lips. He pulled away just an inch, his beautiful bruised lips opened to speak. "Ana," he whispered, "I'm trying to trust you, too." I pulled his head back down to me to finish our kiss. We both suddenly got lost in each other. His kiss grew more demanding, and we were panting and gripping each other like we couldn't get enough. My hands dug into his shoulders as I tried to urge him closer. He pulled back again, looking at me with dark eyes and lowered lashes. "I can't share you, Ana. I can't." His lips brushed softly against mine. "I won't."

I didn't reply, too drunk on a kiss to form a coherent thought.

He pulled back into the driver's seat as a sobering thought occurred to him. "I know, I'm not being fair. I shouldn't be bringing this up right now. Not with everything going on. I will take you home so you can rest. I'm sure you have a lot to think about."

I pressed the tips of my finger to my swollen lips. "I love you, Hayden." I didn't want him to feel guilty, thinking I was in a vulnerable state. I had wanted him just as much as he had wanted me.

He nodded and drove away and we sat in comfortable silence for a while, each in our own thoughts.

"What is she?" I asked suddenly.

He paused, looking at me. He knew what 'she' I was referring to: my mother. He was watching me, preparing to gauge my expression again. "She's one of us. A Hunter."

I exhaled a shaky breath. "She's a hunter." I wasn't asking for confirmation, somehow I just knew. My mother was a Hunter. My dad was definitely human so that would make me, what, half-blooded? "So I'm half-Hunter?" Did that even exist? Did I have supernatural abilities, then? That wouldn't explain the dreams. Even Hunters didn't have those.

"Ana…"

"Oh, that's right. I won't get any answers from you about the supernatural. Gosh—" I turned to look out the window. "Just don't," I cut him off as he tried to make excuses.

"I don't know everything. If I did, I would tell you. I didn't get much out of your mother until we were called to the warehouse because of the demon."

"Wow." I shook my head, feeling dangerously close to a nervous breakdown. I looked at the clock on Hayden's car. It was just after four in the morning. I was exhausted and had less than twelve hours to get ready for the ball. *The masquerade ball,* I can't believe I was thinking about it at a time like this. "My classmate was possessed, my best friend's a voodoun, and I don't know which is worse, that my mother is actually my history teacher or that she is a Hunter."

Hayden pulled over and put the car in park. "Come here." His voice was soothing, welcoming and promised comfort. I turned into him, sobbing quietly into his leather jacket.

"Hayden?"

"Yes?" He unstuck hair glued to my face from tears.

"Why would a demon want me dead? Do demons and ghosts," I was thinking about the ghost of Delphine Lalaurie who had tried to kill me earlier, "usually go after Hunters?"

I looked up at him and his expression turned stony. His beautiful emerald eyes had hardened. "It's always the other way around."

Chapter Twenty Two

✤

S omewhere on the drive home, I had fallen asleep. I stretched my arms out on either side of me, fighting the fog from sleep. I tried to kick off the tangle of covers that had entwined around my body when I noticed the familiar dark bedspread. I was in Hayden's room. I smiled at the fact that he'd brought me to his own bed instead of mine. It was such a protective move that I couldn't stop it from pulling at my heart strings.

I looked over at the clock and shot out of bed at the time. *I had been sleeping most of the day!* I gave Hayden's room one last smile and then slipped out into the hallway. I heard voices downstairs but I first ran into my bathroom. I could only imagine what an all-nighter, demons, and crying did to Nikki's make-up job.

After I washed up and thoroughly brushed my teeth, I headed back to Hayden's room to get a shirt from his closet. After donning one of Hayden's oversized — and very comfortable — shirts, I took a deep breath and headed downstairs.

Even before I got to the bottom, I knew what I'd find: Hayden, Luke, my mother, and Hayden's parents all sitting, waiting for me, in the living room. My heart beat rapidly, and I hated how everyone knew it.

"Adriana," Rachel was the first one to greet me.

"It's Ana…"

"That's not what I named you."

I snorted and was about to retort when I saw the faces of everyone else in the room. They had fallen silent, which was unusual, especially for Luke. And they all held the same grim expression. "What?" I asked Hayden. He just looked behind me at Rachel.

"We need to talk. I know you must have so much you want answered."

My jaw slackened at her words. *We need to talk.* That sounded like a command and I, for one, didn't like to bossed around. *I know you must have so much you want answered.* It was so assumptive, so egotistical. She was the one who had left me, so, yeah, I wanted answers. Hell, I deserved answers. "Let's just get this straight right now: my curiosity for what I am is the only thing that's keeping me here right now. Otherwise, I wouldn't give you one minute of my time."

"You're angry."

Obviously!

I didn't reply but must have rolled my eyes or scoffed my answer because she took a pleading step towards me. "Adriana, please. I didn't have a choice. I did what I did to protect you."

"*Protect* me? You have *no* idea how tired I am of everyone trying to protect me. In case you haven't noticed, I have been just fine for the past seventeen, almost eighteen, years!"

She looked down with a swallow. "If I had stayed, I would have lost you again."

"Again? What do you mean again?"

She deflected my question. "You are almost eighteen, now. And that's when we would have been reunited. Obviously, under present circumstances," she looked at the Boudreauxes "that time had to come earlier. I am sorry you had to find out this way. It's not how I thought it would happen, believe me."

I shook my head, too confused to make sense of anything she said.

"But I do suppose Hayden and Luke served their purposes; you got to be introduced to Hunters and see what it's like first-hand," she added.

A knot twisted in my gut at the way she talked about them in past tense. I cocked my head at her. "So I'm half-Hunter."

She laughed like what I said was humorous. It wasn't funny in the least! "No, you are completely, 100% a full-blooded Hunter."

"My father is a Hunter, too?" *How did I not know that?* "And why didn't he say anything to me about you? Y'all have to have seen each other on multiple occasions, and he never even batted an eye."

"Your father didn't recognize me, because he's not your father."

I heard a gasp from Elizabeth and sound from Hayden, even. It was becoming clear that they were just finding out this information as it was being revealed to me. I felt the air leave my lungs and then everything started to become dizzy. My skin tingled, especially the tips of my fingers, and I started seeing spots. That's when I remembered to breathe. I felt Hayden behind me, keeping me upright like he always did.

"I'm sorry, Adriana," Rachel was even more pleading and even more sincere.

"How?" I managed to choke out.

"Your real father was a great man, he loved you very much."

There she went again, deflecting and speaking in past tense. Why would she tell me my real father loved me very much? Yes, my dad wasn't perfect, but he did love me. All my childhood memories flashed before my eyes and I let out a whimper as the tears came. What made me cry harder, was when I realized that it explained why he had alienated me for his new family. Maybe he just realized what he had been missing when he had a child from his own blood? It could explain why we were so distant these days. I gripped my chest. It hurt *so* badly there, I thought the pain would overcome me, that I would just burst into a million pieces. That my heart would just stop beating from the pain. But it didn't. And I was still there, in a room, with the mother I had wondered about my whole life, who just shattered my old life to pieces.

I had basically been living a lie. I was a lie. I was not my father's daughter. I touched my hair, as if a thought occurred to me. My father had a head full of straight, dark hair. My new mother, a mousy brown which she now wore down in a more stylish manner. She had also had ditched her glasses, which, of course, being a Hunter, she never needed in the first place. Hayden tightened his arms around me.

"All right, let's give her a break," Hayden spoke resentfully from behind me. How was I even able to continue standing upright? Why hadn't I just had a nervous breakdown and completely lost it yet?

Rachel straightened her stance in defiance, and her chin titled up in an aristocratic manner. She looked at me, "Adriana, just think, you can get on with your real life this much sooner."

I came out of my reverie. "This is my life."

She shook her head, patronizing me. "No, it's not. This is the life I created for you. So you would be safe until your eighteenth birthday."

"I meant my life now, here with the Boudreauxes." I looked at Elizabeth, Christopher, even Luke. "They are my family now. Even my "fake" father is, despite what you say. Now, if you'll excuse me, I have to get ready for the dance."

I numbly looked away from her.

"Adriana, you can come home now. You don't need to worry about packing anything. I have everything you need on our plantation."

Plantation? Our plantation? A plantation was a mansion. Was she serious? I looked at her and her expectant eyes confirmed that she was merely waiting for me to go with her.

"You can't just come into my life and expect me to change everything!"

"Adriana…" she said in that familiar, scolding tone only a mother could use.

"I'm staying here," I warned her.

"You are just going to throw me out of your life?"

I looked at her with a narrow gaze, wanting to say something to hurt her they way she had hurt me. But I couldn't. "No, I really hope that we can have a relationship, but right now I have a lot of things I just can't move past. And it's not helping that you keep ignoring my questions. You won't tell me what you're protecting me from, why my father took me in if he wasn't really my father…"

"I will explain everything, I promise. Right now I just want to take you home where we can discuss this in private." Her eyes darted briefly to Hayden, as I was still in his arms.

"This is her home, too. I love Ana." I looked behind me at Hayden whose expression was stormy.

"I love her, too. And to hell if I'm going to let someone else try to take her from me, even if you are her mother, which I'm pretty damn suspicious of right about now. Pretty convenient, you just show up after people make two attempts on her life and try to whisk her away."

Luke. All of a sudden, no one was quiet. Even Christopher stood up protectively.

Rachel clapped her hands together with a laugh. "Oh, boys. Of course you love her, she is your queen. But unfortunately for you, this queen already has a king."

I rolled my eyes. Why was everyone bringing that up? Why was everyone making a big deal about the school dance and being queen?

I looked at Hayden questionably. His head was hung, his expression pained. "Hayden?"

Then I knew Rachel wasn't referring to the school dance.

"Christopher? Elizabeth?" I looked at Hayden's parents. They knew, too. And it became obvious by their faces that this wasn't a good piece of information.

"What the hell is that supposed to mean?" Luke was the only one who seemed to be as clueless as I was.

Hayden backed away from me now until we were no longer touching. "How did I not know this?" He was talking to Rachel.

"You didn't know what she was because I did my job and made sure she remained well-hidden until the time came when all of her traits would return to her."

"Her eighteenth birthday."

"Right, but for some reason her relationship with other Hunters, i.e. the two of you," Rachel pointed to Luke and Hayden spitefully, "caused some of those traits to surface sooner, like the dreams."

"How do her psychic dreams have anything to do with being a Hunter?" Luke questioned.

Rachel gave a look to Christopher and Elizabeth. "Have you not taught your boys anything?" I kind of resented her for saying that. Elizabeth was a great mother. "While Hunters are only called during or after a supernatural creature upsets the balance, only members of the royal family are able to predict such a thing *before* the crime is actually committed. Thus preventing travesties before they're too late."

Luke was still skeptical. Hayden suddenly seemed distant and Christopher and Elizabeth wouldn't even look at me. I just stood there while everyone was talking about me, not to me.

"We are very sorry, your majesty. We didn't know," Christopher spoke solemnly.

Rachel brushed him off coolly. "No harm done. She was almost killed a few times in your care but I'm willing to look past it now that I've had to step up."

I blanched. *What?*

"I can't give her up," Hayden whispered harshly to his father.

"Hayden..." Christopher warned.

"To hell if I'm going to let Little Miss Teacher come in here and change everything," Luke announced loudly.

"I'm sorry," Elizabeth was talking to Rachel, with fear in her kind eyes, "he's only been returned to us since his parents were destroyed. He doesn't know."

"Well, let me put it to you straight." Rachel took a seething step toward Luke. "First of all, *I* am her mother. And to give you a quick history lesson, you are here because of me. The royal family created you and we also have the power to destroy you. That means I am your superior, and you will obey me one way or another."

Luke scoffed, clearly not caring about the second part of her argument and I just loved him all the more for that. "Yeah, where were you the past eighteen years? Where were you during our so called 'failed attempts' at protecting her?"

Rachel was in front of Luke in a flash.

"Wait!" Seeing someone's life in danger finally gave me the courage to speak. "Hello? I am right here and I am tired of you speaking for me. Rachel, you're right, we do need to talk privately. I have even more questions than I had before." I shook my head in wonderment as I thought about this new world Rachel just painted for me. She really wasn't referring to Mardi Gras Queen. I couldn't possibly be Queen of the Underworld? *'This queen already has a king.'* She had to be kidding, right? Even more, she wanted to take me away from everything I'd known. For some reason, in all my fantasies of finding my mother, I'd always pictured her fitting perfectly into my life, not me having to fit into hers. Although I wanted to run away, or to tell her to 'leave me alone' like the sullen teenager I should have been, I was hesitant. The power she seemed to have over everyone, sans Luke, surprised me. And scared me. "Apparently, you want me to just start this new life with you and, I'm sorry, it isn't that easy." I swallowed. "It's not like you are going to force me to come with you. Are you?" I added suspiciously.

She pushed her lips into a thin line. "No, Adriana. I can't force you," she said with a practiced calm.

I exhaled a surprising breath of relief and nodded. "Please, just go home. I will call you tomorrow, after the ball, and we can talk about everything then."

Everyone was looking at me like I had said something taboo. And I met their glances with a questionable one of my own. With fearful eyes, Elizabeth willed me to stop. Were they really that afraid of Rachel? What loyalty did they have to her? I looked at Hayden, who didn't reveal one ounce of emotion, then back at Rachel. Her eyes closed briefly before flashing back open with sadness. She turned on her heel and walked toward the door. "You are so much like your father." The door slammed shut behind her.

Everyone immediately relaxed when she left.

I gave Hayden a look that said he owed me one heck of an explanation.

"Go ahead, Hayden. We need to have a little talk with Luke, anyway," Christopher said after reading my expression.

Hayden gave a curt nod to Christopher before turning back to me, "Let's talk upstairs." He held out his arm for me to lead and I hated the way he deliberately avoided touching me.

The ding of the door bell halted our ascent. "I'll get it," I said with a little irritation in my voice that my mother had returned so soon.

Hayden's ear titled toward the door, "It's not your mother."

"Human?"

He nodded.

"I'll get it," I said again. My mind was going over the possibilities of who it could be as I opened the front door. "Marie," I smiled at the nice surprise.

She returned my smile. "Hi. Were you expecting somebody else?"

"Kind of. Sorry, long story." My eyes darted to the garment bag she held in her arms. "Do you want to come in?"

Her eyes floated behind me to Hayden who was still on the stairs. "I'd better not." Her answer gave me more questions.

"Why not?" More surprising was that she didn't seem to have any questions for me. Like she already knew. I hadn't had the chance to talk to her since I'd confirmed she was a voodoun.

"Are you still going to the ball?" She ignored my question and it was becoming increasingly difficult to read her.

"Yes, are you?" We were still standing in the doorway.

She nodded. "I wanted to bring this over to you." She held out the garment bag for me to take. When I didn't reach for it, she added, "I know we talked about this and I know you said you won't wear it, but I'm giving it to you anyway."

"Marie, I can't," I shook my head, "it's like a family heirloom." The dress was in the chest that was passed down to her from her grandmother. I couldn't wear something that was so valuable to her. It was practically an antique.

"The dress is yours. I mean, it literally belonged to you."

"I think I would have remembered owning a dress like that."

"You know exactly what I mean, Ana."

And I did. Because something about the way she said that the dress was mine reverberated in me. I was comfortable with her statement, like I knew that it was true. It just seemed… familiar.

"How?"

"Just take the dress, Ana."

I nodded and took it, a little shocked from her command.

"See you tonight." She started to leave my front porch.

"Marie?" I stopped her.

"Yeah?" She paused, turning back around.

"Nothing's changed between us, right?" I was suddenly afraid of losing her. Just when our friendship was getting going, it had become awkward between us and for some reason I thought it was because she knew about my Hunter blood. I wanted to be there for her. I knew she was going through a lot, discovering who, or what, she was. Even though I was now going through the same thing, I still wanted to help her figure it all out.

"No, nothing's changed."

As she was walking away, I was hoping that that was true.

Hayden was still waiting for me when I got back inside.

If something from Marie and I's conversation showed on my face, Hayden didn't comment on it. Instead, he just followed me upstairs where we could talk in relative privacy.

"Why didn't you stand up for me?" I jumped right in to what hurt me the most.

"Ana, she's your mother. It wasn't my place."

"No, it wasn't just that. It was something more. Like when she told you who she was. When she told you that I would be Queen."

"Your mother is basically a ruler in the underworld. In all my years, I have never seen anyone go up against her. Or, at least, no one has lived to disobey her. Especially not Hunters. What you are is far more than I could have ever imagined."

"So, what, we can't be together?" I said jokingly, but then saw his face. "What? We can't be together?"

Tears blurred my vision before I knew it.

Hayden quickly rubbed my shoulders, shushing me. "I didn't say that. There just a few more… complications."

"Why are you avoiding touching me?" I noticed how he didn't hold me, rather just comforted me at the bare minimum.

He dropped his arms and turned away so I couldn't see his face. "Ana, that's ridiculous."

"No, it's not. Look at you, you can't even say that to my face."

His back remained toward me.

"Is it true, then, there's something about me being a princess, or whatever I am, that is why you love me?" The realization hit me like a bucket of ice water.

When Hayden turned around, his green eyes were fierce. "I've loved you from the first moment I saw you. When you were just Adriana Alexander. Human. Not a future queen."

The edges of my heart burned. I felt like there was a lingering *but* to his statement.

But we can't be together. *But* this isn't going to work out. *But* your mother will destroy me if this continues. That was what he was going to say, wasn't it? Wasn't that the reason he had become so cold toward me? Why he barely touched me?

"Then kiss me, Hayden."

"Ana," he looked to the heavens, struggling with something internally.

"Kiss me!" My voice shook with anger, fear and desperation.

When he looked back at me his eyes had fire in them. He closed the distant between us, covered my mouth with his, and gave me a quick, punishing kiss. He pulled back only to look at me. His dark hair was disheveled from my hands, his lips bruised from my kiss. "Nothing, and no one, can change how I feel about you."

I nodded as he released me.

"You'd better get dressed if you are still bent on going to the school dance."

I nodded. He left me alone in my room with my thoughts and one heavy, Victorian dress.

Chapter Twenty Three

❧

W hen I finally finished struggling to get into the dress, I looked over my work in the mirror. The dress was even more beautiful than I remembered when I first saw it that night at Marie's. There was just one thing missing.

The mask.

Laying on my bed was a matching half-mask. It was beautifully detailed with dark purple and black mesh fabric against a silver background. The silver peeked through just enough to make it sparkle. It had a black velvet trim with peacock feathers accentuating the right side. I picked up the mask, admiring the enchantment and mystery that came with it.

"I guess it's true, then."

I turned around to find Luke leaning against my doorway.

"What's true, then?" I said with a childish stubbornness, too curious to remember that I was supposed to be ignoring him.

"It doesn't matter what you wear, I simply won't be able to keep my hands off you." His gaze raked the length of my body and suddenly the layers of the dress felt entirely too hot.

I swallowed, fighting the smile that was threatening me. Why did it have to be Luke that was the only one who didn't act any differently toward me?

I turned back around, facing the floor-length mirror. It wasn't helping that I could still see him in its reflection, but I had to continue my plan to avoid him.

"Back to giving me the cold shoulder, huh?"

I put the mask over my eyes and tied the black satin ribbon behind my head. I had hoped that the mask could help hide some of my emotions.

"I need to talk you." Luke was more serious now; gone were his charming, indifferent ways.

"I have nothing to say to you," I said as I smoothed out my hair. When I finished, I picked up my skirts and turned toward the door to leave.

As I tried to walk past Luke out the door, he grabbed my arm. "Ana," he pleaded.

His eyes dipped to my chest that was rising and falling with ragged breaths. I needed to leave immediately. "Let me go, Luke." I pulled my arm free, physically able to do so with a strength I didn't know I had. Luke looked at me with wide eyes filled with awe—and desire. I whipped away, fleeing down the stairs, a trail of skirts behind me.

When I got downstairs and far enough away, I pressed my back against the hallway wall to catch my breath. With my palms flat against the wall behind me, I squeezed my eyes closed against intrusive thoughts. My body had betrayed me once again. This had to stop right now. Things were complicated enough with Hayden as it was. But while my mind was telling me one thing, my body was doing something completely different. Now I just had to figure out which side my heart was on. So long as I could help it, I would stick to the plan. Out of sight and out of mind, right? It was one of the many reasons I was thankful that he would not be coming along tonight.

"Are you sure you want to do this?"

I looked up at Hayden, feeling even guiltier as I saw the concern in his handsome features. Hayden looked powerful and confident in a black suit, black vest, with a dark purple ascot tie that matched my dress. His hair was slicked back in a way that, combined with the suit, made my stomach flutter.

"This is a normal high school dance, for normal high school students, who do normal high school things. I can do this, okay?" My voice sounded a little more panicked than I wanted.

Hayden chuckled. "All right." Hayden held out his arm. "Shall we?"

I nodded and linked my arm in his.

He leaned over, burying his nose in my hair. "You look beautiful. " The heat of his breath on my neck caused me to shiver. Hayden led me away from the garage to the front door.

"Where are we going?"

Before he could reply, he opened the front door where a man was waiting patiently on the porch. His posture was erect, and he was wearing a suit which didn't match how young he looked. I'd seen him before in passing around the house and knew he worked for Hayden, although I didn't know what he did.

"Mr. Boudreaux, Miss Alexander," he gave us a curt nod.

"Troy," Hayden greeted back. That is when I noticed the car parked in the front of our circular driveway.

"Hayden…" I tried my best to scold him. "I said *normal*."

He gave me an impossible look. "This isn't normal? I thought students took limousines to dances."

"I'll take your word for it."

"You've never been before?"

"Not really."

"Why start now?" He said, like he already knew the answer.

Yes, a part of me was going for the wrong reasons. But also I just wanted to have fun and forget about everything else. I could feel things were changing. Whereas I used to embrace my differences while longing for something more, I was now desperately trying to cling to the stability of my former self, my life before all of this.

"Maybe I just want to show you off," I teased.

He pulled up one side of his kissable lips. "Believe me, that pleasure is all mine." Troy opened the door to the limo and Hayden helped me—and my skirts—inside. Hayden slid in beside me and the door was shut behind him.

It was quiet and pleasant inside, like we were in our own little room. The black leather was comfortable and the mood-lighting calming. This was the second time I had ever been in a limo. The first was when I was caught by a rival gang of mortal Hunters called the Vasquez. I'd endured a seven-hour drive in a limo with four of them. I had been hit on, insulted, and threatened. It was the worst day of my life. I thought I would die that day, but it turned out that would be the first of many times I would think that. I looked over at Hayden, feeling uneasy from the memories. I felt the car start moving.

"You okay?"

I swallowed, feeling a little ill. "Just bad memories."

"The Vasquez?" Of course he had figured it out.

"It's no big deal." I brushed it off.

"I'm sorry; I shouldn't have arranged this." He remained where he was, perfectly still except for a scowl on his face, and I found myself hoping he would put his arms around me. He still was cautious with me and I hated that. Ever since he found out what I was.

"Make me forget, Hayden." I didn't know where this wickedness inside me came from. It was entirely new to me and just as shocking to Hayden.

He leaned toward me but it was too late— I had seen him hesitate. I leaned back in my seat, heartbroken.

"Stop." He looked at me with a groan. "I can sense your pain."

"You can *sense* my pain?" I mocked.

"Yes, every emotion is distinct. I can tell when your joy, fear, pain…"

"It doesn't take supernatural instincts to know that I'm hurt, Hayden," I scoffed.

I could feel his eyes burning into me but I kept staring straight ahead, refusing to look at him. Because he still hadn't closed the gap between us and even though I could tell he was longing to touch me, he didn't.

"You're going through a lot right now—"

"What does that have to do with us?"

My eyes slid closed and a tear was forced out. It slid down my cheek, veiled from my mask. "I get it." I had become numb; emotionless and calm. "You think I'm vulnerable?"

⚜

"Why are we here?" I looked at Hayden, wondering if this was some kind of joke or if he really just had something else planned for us.

We were pulled up out front of the Le Petite Theatre Vieux Carre.

"The ball..." he looked at me suspiciously.

"I just thought it would be held at school."

"The gym at Ecole is still under renovation since Katrina—is everything okay?"

"Yes," I nodded, recovering from my shock. "Of course. I was just surprised, that's all."

He pressed a button on the console above him, "Give us a minute, Troy." He looked back at me. "Are you sure?"

Was it too much to hope that this was a coincidence? Probably not. But what else could we do? Go home, and let the underworld, once again, dictate our lives? Or possibly leave my entire class vulnerable to a ghost? No, it would definitely be better if we were there. In case Christine decided to pay a visit again...

"Are you worried about your dream with Christian's murder?" Hayden's words brought up another predicament. He didn't realize I had already been to this theatre. Both in my dreams and in real life after trying to investigate what it was trying to tell me. No, he was referring to the dream I had of the ball, where Luke ended up murdering Mr. Christian.

Were the two related? "Um, yeah," I said, distracted.

He nodded. "We've sorted this out. Christian won't be anywhere near here and neither will Luke. Ana, I won't let anything happen. "

Although his words were comforting. He still had yet to touch me or hold me. I didn't even think to share with him the connection I'd made with the two dreams. It was a completely foreign feeling to me as I had always told Hayden the first thing in my mind. But suddenly, the distance between us that I felt earlier seemed to magnify.

I exhaled. "I know," I nodded, trying to convince myself. "Let's go." I was glad Hayden couldn't see behind my mask. I knew now that in the underworld there were no coincidences. And I may be walking into a trap but what else could I have done? Run away? I couldn't do that anymore. I had to figure it out. Somewhere inside me, I was a Hunter and the very definition of a hunter is to search for, to pursue.

Chapter Twenty Four

✠

W hat a disaster.

I was walking in one of the most beautifully decorated, historic theatres in the world, holding the arm of the greatest guy in the world. I was at my school's masked ball, about to meet my best friends, and I was dressed like a queen. It should have been the perfect evening. Except, everything felt like it was crashing down. The "beautifully decorated theatre" was haunted, the guy whose arm I was holding was cold to me, at least one of my best friends was a voodoun, and Queen? Well, I was just informed that I was a full-blooded hunter and Queen of the Underworld.

Ugh.

I forced a smile as I walked by a group of familiar students, desperately trying to hang on to the first illusion. That I was just at a normal school function, with my normal friends and my normal boyfriend.

I could hear my heart pounding in my ears and I took a few deep breaths to slow my heart beat. Hayden looked at me uneasily and I turned my attention away from him and towards the scene around me.

I needed to appreciate this.

I loved the decorations. The dark blue and white scarves that hung from the ceiling gave the theatre a darkly romantic feel. There were round tables with matching tableware in the same colors in the lobby. A small stage they had set up was empty; most of the tables were, too, and we passed by them as we walked out to the populated courtyard. Music streamed through the French doors and I saw the sway of fine gowns and tuxedos. The courtyard had been rearranged since I had been here a few days ago. Room was made for dancing and garden benches lined with ivy and flowers were set up. Lanterns lined the balcony and starry lights lit the plants. I looked straight up to the dark blue sky, the perfect backdrop and the perfect weather for a night like this.

I wanted to enjoy this but no matter how hard I tried I just couldn't shake the nagging feeling. This evening was supposed to be *fun*. It wasn't supposed to be about anything supernatural. No hunters, no voodouns, no ghosts. Just Hayden, Nikki, Marie and I as normal students.

Hayden and I stopped walking when we got inside the courtyard. I looked at the intimate embrace of couples dancing to the gentle fusion of jazz and modern singing. I smiled longingly then shifted uncomfortably next to Hayden. "I'd better find Nikki and Marie," I said after Hayden stood there, seeming completely unaffected by the silence between us.

He nodded and I left, weaving through students until I caught a glimpse of familiar dark hair.

"Ana!" Nikki called out from behind me just as I reached Marie. I turned around to find her in the arm of a freshman and looking well into her twenties in a purple sequined gown with black smoky eyes behind a matching mask.

I hugged her, my heart swelling with pleasure. "You look gorgeous!"

"Oh this old thing?" She mockingly waved the compliment away with her hand. And I smiled, happy that she was happy. "Look at you, are you kidding me? How you managed to make a creepy antique dress gorgeous is beyond me!"

I elbowed her. "It's *not* creepy." Then I leaned toward her to whisper, "I see you've found a date."

She shrugged, with a secret smile. "Marie!" she remembered, and we both turned toward her talking to a group of people.

Now, Nikki leaned into me. "Wow, voodoo looks good on her."

I elbowed her playfully again. But she was right. Marie looked *new*. She wore her hair up elegantly and a simple white floor-length gown. The only jewelry she wore were dangling chandelier earrings that complimented her bare neck. It was the boldest outfit I had even seen her wear but, most of all, she looked confident in it.

I smiled at Nikki's comment.

"Hey y'all." She hugged us both at the same time.

Nikki felt the skirt of Marie's dress, "I love this."

"You look beautiful, Marie," I agreed.

"Thank you, you guys!" she beamed, definitely not looking like she had just destroyed a demon the night before. "I see you rounded up a date, Nikki! And here I thought we were all going as friends." Marie pointed a look at the tall boy behind Nikki with sandy blonde hair.

Nikki's mouth popped open to protest.

Marie cut her off. "I'm kidding! It's fine." She turned her attention on me. "Where's Hayden, I thought he was coming?"

I adjusted my mask nervously, grateful that I was wearing it. "He's by the lobby. I just left him to find y'all."

"I heard Stephanie is a no-show!" Nikki changed the subject, whispering conspiringly.

Marie and I just looked at each other wide eyed, forgetting that she hadn't known what happened last night.

Should we tell her? I looked at Nikki who was smiling with childlike joy. I shook my head inconspicuously at Marie. Nikki should just be able to enjoy her night and not have to have that plague her thoughts like it was plaguing mine.

"Y...Yeah, well that will be good for our next Queen," Marie recovered.

"Queen?" A sophisticated voice joined our conversation.

We turned toward the sound.

"Oh, hi Miss Vitale," Marie didn't miss a beat.

Nikki gave a tight smile, then looked back at me with wide eyes. I could just hear her asking why a chaperone was interrupting our fun. She didn't know who she was, she just thought she was some teacher. *Of course, why would she think otherwise?*

I swallowed and looked at Rachel. "What are you doing here?" I wondered what happened to the "time to adjust" I thought she'd given me. And I was a little annoyed that I now had something else to keep from Nikki.

She gave me an innocent smile, "I'm chaperoning."

Oh. So when she left my house earlier, she already knew she would be at the dance tonight.

I blew out a breath and Nikki looked at me funnily. Clearly, I was in no position to argue with her. "Nice to see you again," I tried to dismiss her.

She ignored my send-off and asked, "Are you girls having a good time?"

My heart twinged a little, it was something a mother would say. I thought maybe I had been too hard on her. *No, not after every-thing.*

"Yes, ma'am." Marie answered for us. "I'm going to get some-thing to drink, does anyone want anything?" Marie asked Nikki and I. Was she intentionally making her escape? She was unread-able, I couldn't tell.

I frowned. "No, thank you Marie."

"Nikki won't you join me?"

"No, thanks. What? Ow—ohh... Yes, I am actually quite thirsty." Marie was standing a little too close to Nikki and I knew at some point during her words Marie must have pinched her arm. I shot them both a traitorous look and then watched as Nikki followed Marie, happily walking away, with a little too much re-lief.

When they had successfully crossed the courtyard to the lobby, I saw a smile tug on Rachel's lips. "I've always liked her."

I titled my chin. "So have I." I knew she was being nice, but the way she said it had so much more meaning.

"Adriana..."

There she went again...scolding me.

I let out an exasperated breath. I was getting tired. She looked down at her feet, letting the aura of power that was her true self slip and leaving her looking wounded.

"So…" I looked everywhere but her. She would not make me feel guilty.

"I really hadn't planned on coming tonight, even though I wanted to," she gave a nervous laugh. "But they really needed volunteers. I didn't want anything to get in the way of this magical night you're so adamant about having."

I could imagine it was hard to understand why this was so important to me. When you are immortal—and royalty, I can imagine how irrelevant it all could seem. Then I thought of Hayden. He understood. I looked to where I had left him by the lobby only to find he was no longer there. My heart sped up as I looked around the room for him.

Rachel picked up on that. "See, Adriana. This infatuation you have with each other isn't going to last forever. That's why I want you to come home. We've wasted enough time."

My throat ached. "You don't know Hayden."

"But I know you."

I whipped toward her, "Do you?"

"Yes, I do."

"You know me under false pretenses. You aren't the person I thought you were and neither am I."

"It was the only way I could stay close to you and still keep you safe. Do you know how hard it was for me to be in your life but not really *in* your life?"

"Do you know how hard it was for me to not have a mother? Oh wait, you did know, because I told you nearly everything." I looked around me, hoping no heads were turned because of my outburst. Couples continued to glide to the euphoric jazz, booming from the speakers around the courtyard. I turned toward the sound of laughter that was coming from a group of students and teachers alike. No one had heard our disagreement; no one seemed bothered by anything at all. They were just happy. I turned back to Rachel, biting my lips to keep it from quivering.

"Adriana..." her voice was calm and controlled. "You have no idea what's at stake. Everything I did, I did to protect you. You are royalty. There are many people who want you dead, who would love to see our family fall."

I flinched. It was never easy hearing that there were people that wanted you dead. "The Vasquez?"

"I am talking about the entire Underworld. Well, the rogues at least. The ones who don't want to coexist with humans. The ones who are at a great disadvantage if someone predicts their transgressions before they happen and is able to stop them."

"So being a princess or queen—or whatever I am-- there will always be people after me?" I had come to accept that already. When we thought I was human, Hayden told me that being with him would mean people would want us apart.

Her lips quirked. "Well, we are not completely defenseless."

"Ha."

"And I can teach you. I can train you to use your skills so you will be completely untouchable."

"Like you?" I asked carelessly and adjusted my mask. I couldn't believe we were having this conversation here.

"There are people after you, Adriana. People are finding out about you thanks to the Boudreaux. Pretty soon it won't just be one diving accident here and there. It will come at you full force."

"What do you have against them?" I studied her. "And yes, the dive accident. Where were you then?"

"You have to know I would never truly let anything happen to you. Luke was there."

"Oh, so they are only good enough when it comes to protecting me?" I scoffed mockingly.

"Think about how you felt underwater that night. Scared. Helpless. Hoping for a savior?"

My forehead creased as I thought about it. She was right. I felt defenseless. And I hated it.

"You will never have to feel that way again."

I looked away, running my fingers across the leaves of the nearest fern. "I'm not sure." I couldn't stay angry with her forever. But in a way I was not yet ready to forgive her, either.

"I could help you and you could help me."

I looked at her, her brown eyes looking surprisingly vulnerable. "Help *you*?" How would I be able to help her?

"You could help me be a mother again…"

My heart leaped. How long had I wished to hear that? A sliver of hope started to form inside me. I could live with her and still go to school and see Hayden. We could even ride to school together in the mornings—

"…and stay away from the Boudreauxes."

Wait, what? "What makes you think I'd want that?"

"I'm just trying to do what's best for you."

Just when I thought we were on the same page… just when I thought things were starting to mend…"I am *so* tired of arguing about this. Hayden was here for me when you weren't. I love him and I won't abandon him."

She looked at me with the same amount of stubbornness I was giving her. "But will he not abandon you?"

I sucked in a breath, gasping like I had just been punched in the stomach. I blinked fast to try to hold back angry tears. I thought of a million retorts but instead I just turned on my heel and walked away. Rachel hadn't stopped me.

I furiously looked around the lobby for Hayden. He had been acting so cold to me and now he had disappeared? *"But will he not abandon you?"* My mother's words haunted me. I finally went back into the courtyard and leaned against a pillar in defeat. I hung my head but refused to shed any tears over the argument with my mother—Rachel. *When had I started to refer to her as otherwise?*

"It's your party, you can cry if you want to," a surprisingly gentle voice beckoned me.

A gasp escaped me and a smile tugged on my lips. "What are you doing here?" My eyes lit up at the sight of Luke in a tux. He was cleaned up, his hat gone and his hair charmingly slicked. With his hat not casting shadows over his eyes, they looked incredibly bright. Flecks of emerald swirled with a honey brown.

"I am hoping your dance card isn't full." He gave me a brilliant, boyish smile.

I snorted. *If I could only find my date.* Then I remembered I didn't want him here. "You promised me you wouldn't be here."

"And *you* promised me that we could be friends and yet you ignore me. I figured this was the only way to get you to talk to me." He was still playful.

Luke. I gave a little sigh. *Stop having a crush on him!* I ordered myself harshly. But like before, just as I was feeling lonely and about to lose it, he was there for me.

He looked down at me in a way that made me hold my breath. "One dance. And then I'll leave."

I looked around the courtyard and into the lobby one last time. My mouth twisted as I thought about it; Hayden was still nowhere to be found.

I shook my head, "I can't."

His smile fell. "Can't or won't?"

"Both." *Where was Hayden to whisk me away?*

"Stop looking for Hayden, he's not here," Luke couldn't hide the irritation in his voice.

"What do you mean he's not here?"

"I saw him rushing out of here before I came."

My throat tightened. "He wouldn't leave me here." He must have had a very good reason.

"I don't care what you are, Ana. My feelings for you haven't changed since I found out what/who you are."

"I wish everyone would just stop telling me how to feel!" My fists were in balls at my side. I was annoyed that the things my mother and now Luke were feeding me contradicted what I knew about Hayden. I knew him, I trusted him. I was tired of doubting it and tired of the struggle between what I saw and how I felt. Because even though I knew Hayden loved me, his actions said otherwise.

"Then don't think," his hand slipped into mine as he pulled me to the dance floor, "just feel." He pulled me flush up against his body and it was the closest we'd been since our kiss.

"Luke…" I protested as one of his hands entwined with mine while the other slid to the small of my back.

"Just one dance," he shushed me, "and then I'll leave."

I looked around me, to the balcony this time. One dance would be harmless. I had yet to sense Christine and Mr. Christian wouldn't be here. My abilities as a Hunter weren't developed yet. Those dreams were probably just a fluke. For the first time in a while, I had hope.

"Just one dance, then I have to find Nikki and Marie."

He looked down at me with a triumphant smile that was dripping with pure male satisfaction.

My fingers dug into his shoulders and he twirled me with him.

A blush spread across my cheeks as I clumsily stepped on his feet. "Sorry. I'm not a very good dancer."

"You don't have to be. All you need is a really great lead. Luckily, I am."

A laugh escaped my lips as he continued to lead us.

"It's good to see you smiling and laughing. I haven't seen that Ana for a while."

Consequently my smile fell. "Yeah, well, there's kind of a lot going on in my life."

He tried to start talking again, but I cut him off, afraid of where this was going. "Did you want to talk or did you want to dance?"

"Both." He gave me that crooked, playful smile again. "The best part of dancing is," then he leaned in to whisper in my ear, "that you can do this."

I tried to pull back, to put space between us but he held me in place with an unrelenting grip.

"You can talk intimately, whisper seductive things into your partner's ear without the room suspecting a thing. You have an excuse to touch each other, to be close, to have your bodies move in unison. And it's all wrapped up in a socially acceptable package."

I swallowed. "Or dancing can be a performance, an act if you will. Giving the ability of the dancer to be someone else if not just for the length of a song. It's also a courtesy, one that when asked of properly should not be refused. Much like a handshake. But when it's over, you part your ways, leaving behind any connection you had with it."

I felt his deep laugh against my body. "But much like other things… you never forget your first dance."

I realized he was right. This was my first dance. And it was supposed to be with Hayden. It was supposed to be *our* first dance. I felt cold as Luke finally released me and stepped back. I looked up at him, my forehead puckered in confusion until I realized the song had ended and our dance was over.

I smoothed out my dress and took a deep breath. "You got what you wanted, now go."

I could tell Luke was stung, probably by the coldness in my tone. "I'll go," he looked at me sideways. "But I am far from having gotten what I wanted."

I exhaled a breath of relief when he easily walked away. I turned to go find my friends when I came face-to-face with Nikki. "Oh hey, I was just going to look for you."

"Found ya first, I was just waiting for you to finish your dance." She waggled her eyebrows at me.

"What? Stop, no. It's not even like that." I had to change the subject. "Where's your date?"

I followed Nikki off the dance floor. "Ugh, don't even get me started. I should have just come alone. He left me and has been dancing with that Bethany from my calculus class ever since!"

"Seriously?"

"Never should have came with a freshman…"

I wrapped an arm around her shoulders and pulled her into a hug. Even though she tried to use humor to cover her hurt feelings, her eyes looked sad. "Screw 'em."

Nikki lifted up an imaginary cup in her hand, "Screw 'em," she said with a nod.

"Where's Marie?"

"She was swept off into the night by a mysterious gentleman."

"Really?" Nikki and I were smiling at each other, excited for Marie and anticipating hearing all about the new guy.

The music died down and we turned toward the DJ. One of the teachers was in front holding up his arms and directing everyone back into the lobby for hors d'oeuvres and the coronation. Nikki gripped my arms and squealed. I smiled, tried to be excited with her but the fact was that even though I was surrounded by a hundred people, I still felt out of place; I felt lonely.

"Why, aren't you just a sight for sore eyes!"

I whipped around at the sound of the warm, southern drawl. "Mr. Christian!" With realization, all the blood drained from my face. "Mr. Christian..."

He wrapped his arms around me in a hug and pressed a scratchy kiss to my cheek as I stood there paralyzed in fear. Why was Mr. Christian here? He wasn't supposed to be here.

"What— are you doing here?" I realized that was the third time I'd asked that question to someone tonight.

"You ain't happy to see me?" He laughed heartily, "I'm teasin'. Didn't your dad tell ya?"

"Tell me what?"

He put his arm around me, "the school called him looking for volunteers to help out with this but he had to watch Brittany last minute so he asked if I could come for him. Since you have been saving my behind at the dive shop, I thought this was the least I could do to repay you. Besides, I didn't want to miss seeing you in dress."

"Hi, I'm Nikki, Ana's friend." Nikki saved me by cutting in and taking over with her mega-watt smile and relaxed charm.

While Mr. Christian and Nikki talked, I studied him in horror. His face was lit up in innocent joy. He'd even cleaned up, wearing a brown suit and suede shoes. He had a *"Hi, I'm Christian"* name tag on his chest. Written underneath his name in bold, taunting letters read "volunteer".

No, no. This was fine. It would be okay. I nodded to myself. Luke had left. I would send Mr. Christian away, it *will* be fine.

"Let's go, I want to get a good table." Nikki tried to rush us into the lobby.

"Wait!" I inappropriately cried out, then managed to prevent my hand from clamping over my mouth at the outburst. "I mean. Mr. Christian—you don't have to stay, really its fine. It looks like they have more than enough volunteers helping out." I put my hand around his back and tried to move him toward the other exit.

"Aw, I don't mind, sweetheart. It looks like a good time anyhow."

Okay, so he wasn't leaving with any subtleness.

"Yes, and you have to stay and see Ana crowned Queen."

I groaned internally but refrained from shooting Nikki a look since she didn't know what had happened in my dream.

Christian turned to me looking at me with a renewed brightness in his eyes. His mouth was popped open in a silent gasp. "Now I wouldn't miss that for the world! Your dad didn't tell me nothin' about that."

I brushed it off and tried to move him along. "Oh, it's nothing really. Nothing is for certain. Besides, it's going to be boring. A lot of waiting around and long speeches."

"I don't mind really, thanks for looking out for me though." And then he immediately started walking to the lobby with Nikki.

I hesitated, out of shock, and then struggled to keep up. *This couldn't be happening.* "Mr. Christian, I don't really think it's a good idea."

Nikki looked at me quizzically over her shoulder. I tried to warn her but Mr. Christian ignored my protests and held out an arm for Nikki to link with.

I took a deep breath to calm my rising panic. What could I do? I couldn't physically force him to leave. *But Hayden could...* I looked around for him, knowing he could help me. I wiped my forehead with my hand when I still couldn't find him. I began to feel a little dizzy. *Marie!* I remembered Marie's newly discovered powers and hoped she could help. I walked around the room this time, zig-zagging through the students waiting to enter the lobby. Why was it that everyone who could help me was missing?

A pang shot through my heart at the realization that Hayden had left me alone. Defeated, I walked in with everyone else, spotting Mr. Christian and Nikki at a table with three other students. I kept watching the room even as I sat. Luke had left. That was the only thing I was relying on.

I tried to return the smile Mr. Christian gave me as the lights dimmed in the lobby and the principal took the stage. After introductions, we had several performances and traditional dancers float by us as we ate. I picked at my dessert, too worried sick to be able to stomach anything. I watched Nikki laugh and Mr. Christian talk to the other staff member at our table, enjoying himself. I kept watching the room, miserably. But as the minutes ticked by I began to relax, wondering if what I really dreamt was right. What if it didn't have anything to do with predicting the future? My mother had said my abilities were slowly coming back. What if I just had a regular nightmare? With everything going on with Luke and my roller coaster of emotions, it was completely possible.

When they called the Court to the stage, I panicked. "Mr. Christian, we have to get out of here."

He patted the hands I had gripped around his arms as I tried to pull him out of his chair. "Don't be nervous, sweetheart."

"Oh no you don't, Ana. We haven't come this far for nothing." Nikki was pulling me away from Mr. Christian to the stage.

"No, Nikki. Something bad is going to happen."

"Nothing bad is going to happen," she chided.

"Nikki, I'm serious!" I said in a low hiss. "I had a dream about it."

She froze and I could see her considering it. She looked back at Mr. Christian and then when she realized the danger I referred to had to do with him, she frowned. "Just go. I will get him out of here."

"I can't—"

"Go! Everyone is waiting for you. I will make him leave."

I looked around. We were stopped in the center of the room, the other students running for King and Queen, sans Stephanie, were already on stage and looking at me expectantly.

"Go, I'll take care of it, I promise." She shooed me away.

"Find Hayden and Marie." I called back to her.

She nodded and I looked back helplessly at her as I picked up my skirts and walked to the stage.

The principal gave long introductions for each of us and I blushed at how good Nikki had made me appear on the application. I shot one last look around the room. Hoping to find salvation. Hoping *not* to find Luke.

I watched Nikki from the stage as she spoke to Mr. Christian. Her hands were flailing about wildly around her in emphasis as she spoke. I had wondered what she said to make Mr. Christian shoot out of his seat. Mr. Christian and Nikki looked around and then Nikki pointed to the courtyard, probably trying to find the best way to exit without disturbing everybody. They squeezed past the chairs of other guests until they got to the walkway by the courtyard. Nikki tried to lead the way out, but Mr. Christian stopped and held up a finger to her indicating she should wait. I gulped as I willed them just to leave already. Mr. Christian turned around with a smile. Taking something small and black from the inside pocket of his brown coat. A camera? He wants to take a picture?

The action of Mr. Christian turning the winding mechanism seemed perpetually slow. Everything seemed to slow down. From Nikki trying to pull on his jacket, to the emcee saying the winner had to be changed because of a no-show. The only thing that seemed to be in normal speed was the appearance of Luke from behind the courtyard pillar. Watching me with pride. "No," I gasped, not caring if the whole world heard. Then Luke's attention turned toward Mr. Christian. He frowned, then his eyes widened. He must have remembered my dream. He turned to leave and that's when I heard the buzzing. There was no mistaking the buzzing noise in my ears, or the slight vibration I felt against my skin. Something supernatural was here.

You know that feeling you get when you know something terrible is going to happen? It's a helpless feeling. It started off with a little pull against my insides. A little nagging feeling that became hard to ignore. But that was earlier in the evening, when I'd had hope, so it didn't take its full form. Standing on stage with my peers as the crown drifted over our heads teasingly before it would land on the winner, I didn't have hope. My ears buzzed and I felt currents vibrating my skin, getting stronger as if the supernatural being was getting closer.

Luke had of course felt it, too, because he paused and his shoulders stiffened. He whipped toward me with a wild look in his eyes. Those wild eyes darted toward Mr. Christian, and where the currents were coming from. "No," I whimpered again, quieter now for his ears only. His eyes came back to me and I felt relief that I hadn't lost him yet. He drew in his brows and even from the stage I could see him clench and unclench his fists. He was struggling with himself. He was fighting the instincts to hunt. I shook my head and pleaded with my eyes. *Go, Luke. Leave.* He closed his eye with agonizing slowness. *Please!* I whispered out loud. Couldn't he do this for me? Couldn't he walk away this time, knowing what the outcome would be if he didn't?

I looked at Mr. Christian hoping to see if Nikki was getting him out of there but I didn't matter now if Nikki did or not. Luke would find him. And he wouldn't stop until he did. It wasn't until I saw the familiar ghost dressed in white that I realized the supernatural vibes weren't coming from Mr. Christian but from Christine, who was looming behind him in the court yard. Then all the pieces came together beautifully. Mocking me for not figuring it out sooner.

I flinched as I felt something in my hair. I looked over my shoulder to see the Principal, resting the crown upon my head. I was Queen.

I turned back to Luke only to find he was gone.

I looked back to Mr. Christian and the ghost that was behind him. She looked at me with a sinister "I told you so" and shook her head disapprovingly at me. I wanted to scream at her, to get out all my frustrations about why this was happening and why I couldn't have figured it out sooner and more importantly, why I couldn't stop it. And that's just what I did as applause broke out in the audience for the new Queen, I screamed. Because Christine now had Mr. Christian elevated, his face frozen in fear as her translucent hands bound around his neck.

I turned to run off the stage to Mr. Christian. A pair of hands caught me before I made the stairs down the stage. I looked up horrified. The lady from the attendance office was now patting my back telling me it was okay and to not be nervous. I felt sick. I wanted to tell her that someone was in danger but my mouth kept opening and closing, no words escaping. I recoiled from her and even then she didn't let go. I looked helplessly at Mr. Christian whose face had become a frightening pale and whose eyes had lost their luster. I looked at Nikki who was the only person who seemed to notice the ghost that was killing someone in the court-yard. Nikki was frozen a few feet away except for sobs that racked her body and the tears that were streaming down her face. I wanted to either tell her to *run* or *help him* but I didn't know which one was more selfish. A glimmer of green caught my attention from besides Nikki. It was a pair of eyes; specifically Luke's, who was in full hunting mode. The green in them looked particularly bright— and murderous. I had never seen him so dangerous, even with the demon the night before, and I realized then what his deci-sion had been. He hadn't chosen me over Hunting. His love for me didn't prevent him from his blood lust. In his right hand held an old iron fire poker.

I took off running, slipping from the attendance woman's grasp, if only for a second. Her hands returned as well as another pair and words from all sorts of people who were hushing me and en-couraging me to not have stage fright. I heard a strange noise and realized that it came from me.

Luke ran toward Mr. Christian and Christine, but instead of the usual blur of his supernatural speed, everything and everyone around us seemed to slow down, and I could actually see him run-ning. I held my breath; the moment he charged toward Mr. Chris-tian with the iron poker, I still had hope that he would save him. That breath exploded when he rammed the poker through Mr. Christian and Christine who was behind him, binding them to-gether.

"No!" With all the strength I had in me, I pushed my arms out. Whoever had been around me was gone now, and I was free. I had taken off toward Mr. Christian when I noticed the flames. Those sitting nearest the courtyard had started to notice them, too, and there were a few screams and sounds of chairs falling back. Where Christine and Mr. Christian had been was now one form on fire. More shouts and chaos had started to form as the fire spread to the ivy. I fought the crowds to make it to the lifeless form. As I was standing in the spot where Mr. Christian had watched me from stage there was no sign of him. Flames started to consume any-thing flammable around me, but Mr. Christian was gone. Not even ashes remained on the floor. I had failed him. I had predicted this and yet I didn't save him. I clawed at my hair as I dropped to my knees and just cried. *Why?* I sobbed. Mr. Christian, one of the kindest, purest-hearted people I knew. He was like my uncle. He was family. *Why?*

I was sweating and I knew it was due to the heat from the fire, yet I couldn't pull myself up to run away. I was empty. Numb. Sui-cidal. *Who cares what happens to me?*

"Adriana." A voice that wasn't shaken nor panicked sounded from beside me.

I turned to the woman kneeling beside me and wrapped my arms around her. "Mom," I cried more until she helped me to a stand. I remembered something and panicked, "Where's Nikki?"

"She made it out with the others, I'll debrief her later."

I stared at the bottom of my dress and the fire that was inching close to it. The brightness was almost enchanting and I couldn't walk away.

"I'm not ready to test your immortality tonight." Rachel was still calm, and collected. "We are leaving. *Now.*" She led me out of the building and I longingly looked over my shoulder at the flames.

Chapter Twenty Five

✦

We were in Rachel's "teacher" car driving who knew where. This wasn't happening. Mr. Christian wasn't dead. He couldn't be dead. There wasn't anything even left of him. He needed a funeral. Zack. *Oh my God!*

"Breathe, Adriana!"

I looked at her suspiciously. And resentfully.

"No, I could not have prevented it." She read my expression.

My features softened. I had no choice but to believe her. I let out another breath and ran my hands through my hair. Something caught on my finger nails and I reached with my right hand to the top of my head to pull the crown off. I looked at it for the first time. Large crystals and amethyst sparkled each time we passed under a street lamp. I threw it in my lap with a laugh. A maniacal, sort-of crazed laugh and I wondered if this was it. If I had really lost it.

"I'm sorry. I am so damn sorry. For everything."

I looked at her blankly. She was right all along. If I had known what I was doing I would have been able to stop it. I could have saved Mr. Christian. It was right then and there that I vowed that this would never happen again. I would never let myself be weak again. I would do whatever it took to save the people in my dreams.

"So where is this plantation?"

My mother looked a little surprised at my response. Apparently she was expecting a fight. But that was the old me.

She nodded in understanding. "We'll stop your house first. You can gather anything you hold sentimental and say goodbye. '

Hayden.

"Hayden is there?" My face scrunched up in pain at the memory of him leaving me there. *He could have stopped Luke if he had been there!*

"I have to tell you. I had given Hayden an ultimatum to force him to leave you at the dance."

"You did *what*?"

"It was wrong and I apologize. I thought I was doing what was best for you." She was concentrating awfully hard on the road.

"It doesn't matter, it's over now. Mr. Christian is dead and there is nothing anyone could have done to prevent. Not Hayden being there, not you being there, not my dad chaperoning instead of him, not Marie being there, not Luke leaving, not if the ball had been at the school instead, not if Nikki got him out of there in time! None of that matters because he died anyway!"

"I'm not being insensitive but you need to know that his life wasn't in vain. Ghosts are territorial. With all the spirits in the building, Christine lashed out. Her mind went back to the night she died and she wanted a male soul to pay for it. She would have destroyed anyone or anything in her way to do so. So it might have been your father's friend, but it could have been your entire class."

"Christine didn't kill Mr. Christian," I ground my teeth together, the rage boiling up. "Luke did."

Rachel didn't even flinch. She nodded, "It's one of the ways to kill a ghost. You have to bind it to a human and kill that human when they are bound." Rachel pulled into the circular driveway and put the car in park. "I'll wait for you here."

"It won't be long," I said simply as I got out and made my way to the front door. As I suspected, Hayden was waiting for me when I came inside.

I kept my eyes trained on the floor. I didn't know what I would find in his eyes and I didn't know what the sympathy or regret would do to my resolve.

"I just came to get a few things and to tell you I am staying with my mother for a while." Was that a sniffle that escaped me?

A pained exhale came from Hayden. "I've failed you."

"It wasn't your fault. It wasn't anyone's fault." *Except Luke's.* My eyes glazed over, staring at the Persian rug in the hallway. "Rachel told me about the ultimatum."

"Hell, if I would have known I'd lose you either way I wouldn't have bothered trying to keep away from you!"

I swallowed at his intensity. "Either way, you thought I was vulnerable. As soon as you found out what I was it was like you wouldn't touch me. Why had me being a Hunter changed things? Did you love me in spite of being a human or did you love me because I was human? I'm still me!" My voice cracked at the last bit and I closed my eyes at my screw up. Stay emotionless. Stay *strong.*

"That's ridiculous, Ana! I was doing it for you! Look at me dammit!" He appeared in front of me where I was standing by the stairs. I looked up, but kept my eyes focused on something behind him because my throat was becoming thick and I was afraid I'd cry. *No tears.*

"When I said I can sense how you feel, I meant it." He went on, "If you were full Hunter, you would have known that, you would have known how I felt about you without me ever having to say a word. I wanted to give you space, I wanted to be with you when you were 100 percent sure that was what you wanted. I want all of you Ana. I want you to want all of me, too. When you become a Hunter your senses are magnified. That goes for your emotions, too. I was afraid that any doubt you felt for us would be magnified. I didn't want you to resent me. I didn't think you were vulnerable, quite the opposite. I didn't want you to resent me because you still have a lot of changes to go through. And what if after going through those changes—I am not the one you want. As your mother said, you are a Queen, I am simply your soldier.

Did he actually doubt my feelings for him? I opened my mouth to protest but he cut me off. "It doesn't matter now anyway. You are going to the plantation and we are leaving New Orleans."

That threw my emotionless faux state out the window. *"What?"*

"We have to leave. We are going back to my parents' in Tampa for a while. What Luke did won't go unnoticed. We need to lay low for a while. New Orleans isn't like it was. It's a more grown-up city now since Hurricane Katrina. We can't get away with what we used to. Even Troy couldn't cover this one up."

"You're *leaving* me?"

One corner of his lip curled up, "I'm not leaving you Ana. I was going to ask you to come with me. You are leaving to your mother's now."

My mouth was open but nothing would come out. "I—"

"It's the right decision." He nodded. Could Hunters cry? Because I thought I saw his eyes glisten. "You deserve that life with your mother. You deserve to be away with all the pain I have caused you."

"Stop it!" I shouted and dared to reach out and put a hand on his shoulder. It was a hesitant touch at first, then it became a stroke and I trailed both hands now down his chest. A deep groan sounded from the back of his throat. "I love you. I really do."

"How come I feel like there is a 'but' attached to that statement?"

"But you're right. I need to figure out things. I can't be the person I was. The girl that was weak, that cried easily and fret over things she could or couldn't change... I need to figure out who I am and what I am capable of."

He bit his lower lip and looked to the heavens with a pained expression. Finally, his head came back down and he nodded. "Fine." He nodded again; I wondered if it was more for himself. "But don't you dare think yourself weak for having a big heart. The girl that cries during those damn puppy commercials but didn't bat an eyelash when I pulled her in my truck and kidnapped her. I fell in love with that girl."

I took a step back from him. "I—I can't. Mr. Christian died!"

"I know. And I am sorry. I am so damn sorry, Ana." He tried to pull me toward him and I fought him. He pulled his arms around me and I beat my fists against his chest and tried to fight the sobbing that was racking my chest. "It's okay."

My protests were muffled. And I relaxed, letting him hold me in mind-numbing bliss for the last time in who knows how long. We stood there for the longest time, perfectly still and silent until I heard the engine of a car pull into the driveway. I pulled back like I had been doing something I shouldn't have been.

"It's just Christopher and Elizabeth."

I nodded. Then wondered if Luke was with them. I wasn't ready to see Luke again. Not yet. When I did I wanted to be ready. I wanted to know how to kill a Hunter because when I saw him again, I would have to kill him.

"I guess this is goodbye." There was an odd detachment from my voice.

He licked his lips sadly. "I will wait for you, Ana. However long it takes. I *will* wait for you."

I looked away from his intense gaze. Hayden gave me the opportunity to respond but I just stood there stupidly until he walked away. He let out a regretful noise as he opened the door, then with no other words the door slammed behind him.

Chapter Twenty Six

❧

"I'll be right out." I called my mother from my cell phone and then left it permanently on the table in the foyer. I walked up the stairs to my room to change out of the dress, knowing I would be more comfortable in jeans for whatever my mother had planned for me. I planned to leave everything behind as I didn't have anything that truly belonged to me except my charm necklace and the journal Hayden had given me.

Every move I made was deliberate and calm. It took all my concentration to place my hand on the railing, lift one foot and set it on the next step, and repeat. *Place hand on door knob, twist gently and push.* I suppose thinking about that was better than letting the flood gates open to all the emotions I had to have in me. My grief for Mr. Christian, my joy for having my mother, my love for Hayden, my hatred for Luke. I was a walking contradiction. I tore my mask off and threw it on the bed. Now if I could just get out of this dress that easily. I reached my arm behind my back, struggling to find the top of the laces. I felt a hand brush up against my skin and the laces slowly being loosened. I spun around to find Luke standing in front of me. *Luke.*

"What are you doing here?" Hatred dripped with each word. He didn't reply, only stalking my every move as I backed up. "Get away from me, Luke." I backed into my dresser. "Leave me alone. My mother is in the car outside." I used her as a warning.

He looked up at me through his eyelashes, his eyebrows were drawn together and he was exhaling forcibly. I didn't at first comprehend this look Luke had on him, and then I understood. He was Hunting. I looked down at his hand in which he held a small vile filled with an amber liquid. I sighed from relief. No weapons, but did Luke really need a weapon? And why did he have what looked like a potion? I turned and ran as soon as it dawned on me.

Luke grabbed my arm before I even took a step. He bent down, pulling me backward over his knee. The cork flew off the vile and he held it to my mouth. "Drink" his voice vibrated. It was like he was possessed.

I pressed my lips together and shook my head, too stunned to speak let alone scream for help.

Luke grabbed my face, forcing my mouth open. The liquid burned as it went into my mouth, somehow working down my throat. I sputtered, trying to spit the liquid out. Luke shut my mouth with his hands. "Swallow," he now instructed.

I shook my head again, tears now spilling down my cheeks. The liquid was burning in my mouth. It was almost as painful as the fact that Luke was trying to kill me.

He growled and I trembled in his arms. His lips twitched but he didn't hesitate before pinching my nose shut. I tried to take a breath but my lungs just constricted without air. The pain in my chest and burning in my mouth was too hard to bear. I moaned from under him, pleading with my eyes to have him release my jaw.

"Swallow first."

The liquid slid down my throat and he let me go, I flew across the room, gasping for air the entire time. I could feel the liquid burn as it went down my throat, and into my stomach. I felt a similar burning sensation through my veins and the feeling spread as it made its way through my blood stream, and finally to my heart.

Epilogue

✤

Damn. This is not how I thought it'd go down. What is this emotion that I feel? Guilt? Remorse? No, how can I feel that when I have the girl of my dreams sleeping on my lap. We are in the backseat, Ana in the middle of Hayden and I as our parents drive us back to the beach house in Tampa. But damn, everyone is pissed at me. Everyone except the only one who matters: Ana. I know I maybe didn't go the best route in getting her to fall in love with me. Forcing her to drink a love potion is pretty unforgivable according to my family. But I couldn't help it. *I love her.* I love her so damn much. I place my arm around her. *She is mine.*

"Get your hands off my girlfriend." Hayden is pissed.

"What?" I try to play it off. "I'm keeping her warm. And I don't know if she would agree that she is your girlfriend anymore."

That pisses him off even more. "The only reason I'm not killing you is because she'd hate me. Although if she wasn't under your spell, I'm sure she'd kill you herself."

"Well more power to ya then." I sneak at glance at our parents who are doing a bad job at pretending not to hear our conversation.

"She will always be mine. It doesn't matter what kind of potion you gave her that will fake these feelings towards you. When she had free will, she chose me."

I shrug slightly, careful not to wake up Ana. He is pissing me off and I can't help but to make him angrier. Now he knows exactly how I felt all those times seeing him with Ana, seeing Ana love him and kiss him. Just the mere memory was enough to drive me insane. "You should be thanking me. If it wasn't for me, she never would have gone with us. She would have stayed in New Orleans and neither of us would have had her."

"You are irritatingly naïve, Luke. It wasn't our decision to make. If she chose to stay, then so be it! It is far better than the fate you bestowed upon her."

"Oh, this is coming from the guy who kidnapped her." Heavy sarcasm.

"That was to keep her safe!"

"And that's what I am doing now. She wouldn't have been safe in New Orleans without our protection. And don't get me started on her mother…"

"All I want to know is what the hell did you have to do to get that potion?" Hayden swore. He must be really losing it.

"None of your damn business. Just be glad that she is with us and we can protect her again."

"Don't think for one second I agree with what you've done, or am grateful whatsoever. I would rather have her in New Orleans alone than in love with you," he spit out the last words.

"If you can't have her then no one can? That's pretty selfish coming from you."

"She is not an object, Luke."

"I don't care, she is mine."

"Don't think for one second I will allow you to bind to her."

"So, what, you're going to just let her remain mortal?"

"Yes. Until, I find a cure."

"There is no cure!" He is in major denial that this is happening.

"I will *never* stop looking for a cure."

Missed *Tempest*? Want more of the Boudreaux brothers? Read on for a preview of *Tempest* in Hayden's POV!

Hayden Boudreaux couldn't decide which was worse— that he was falling in love with a mortal or that the only way to break his family's centuries-old curse would be to kill her. Of all that he was certain was the more time he spent with her, the more he knew he would do anything to protect Adriana Alexander, including sacrificing his eternity. What he wouldn't expect was that Luke - his brother that hated Ana, who wanted to kill her - would decide he would want her as his own.

CHAPTER ONE

"We are such stuff as dreams are made on, rounded with a little sleep"
-*Tempest* by William Shakespeare.

What had I become? I hadn't even bothered paying for the car I was driving. Worse, it was as if I didn't even give the stealing a second thought, like it was second nature to just take and not think of the consequences to others. Wasn't that exactly what the Supernatural thought they were? *Super,* as in superior to the normal, tedious doings of the human world? So what if the entire human world depended on the balance that we as Hunters gave it? What I do is nothing to be proud of. I would never be arrogant about it like some of the others…

My hand clenched the leather of the steering wheel at the thought. It took me a while to get off the main road. Soon, the entrance appeared through the vegetation. This was Louisiana and in swamp territory, what's not there one minute can appear the next. Unfortunately, the same theory applied to the opposite. I turned into the unpaved entrance. The thin, one-lane road was the only thing cutting through the swamp. As I drove, the trees were becoming thicker, almost more sinister, like they knew what the end of this road held. I was almost there, I could smell it. It was the scent of incense, of candlewood, of death.

I pulled in front of the run-down house, barely putting the car in park before running to the front door. I was already doing everything else in supernatural mode, why not go all in? The humor almost led to a smile.

Sansha was at the door before I could give it another thought. She wasn't surprised in the least to see me. Of course not. Giving me her pearl-and-gold smile, she held out the door for me to enter.

I kicked away empty bottles as I walked into her clutter. I would never pretend to understand the supernatural. Although, Sansha *did* chose to live in this modest house and that was something I *could* understand.

I realized that I hadn't said a word of greeting, which may have triggered the intense silence between us. Before I could offer a hello, she spoke.

"I hear you were out of your territory."

"You hear or see?"

She laughed without humor.

"I needed to get away. I think even you could understand that," I offered as an explanation.

She nodded. "Your brother is doing well." I scoffed, because I didn't remember asking about him. "You on the other hand," she continued, while giving me a once-over, "you've really let yourself go, haven't you? What a waste, having a human form!" She laughed with a little more humor this time.

"I was human. This is my form," I bit out. I wondered what she saw in me and I looked down at my bare torso. It was no wonder, I wasn't even properly dressed.

"Mmm," was all she replied as she left me to sit on a chair.

"So, why am I here?" I remembered my human courtesies and sat down across from her.

She regarded me for a while and I was silent, letting her play her games.

Her mouth parted for a while before the words came out, "I think it's time to go back to New Orleans."

"I was just in New Orleans taking care of that vampire situation."

"I meant for good." She leaned back in her chair, her braids thrown over her shoulders. "Are you still planning on destroying yourselves just to break the curse?"

I clenched my jaw and gave her a curt nod. Did everyone know what we were planning? That we would rather not exist at all then have to continue to serve the Underworld?

"What if there was another way? Would you do it? How far would you go to be released from the hold of the Underworld?"

"Anything," I said with slightly more emotion. She already knew the answer.

"Kill?"

I scoffed. Wasn't that what I was created to do?

"A human?"

About the Author

Jenna-Lynne Duncan graduated from the University of St. Thomas with degrees in Political Science, International Studies and Middle Eastern Studies. She is the author of the popular young adult novel *Hurricane,* and the novella *Tempest.* She is currently working on a fourth *Hurricane* novel as well as another YA series. Besides writing, Jenna-Lynne likes children and traveling. Preferably together.

To know more about Jenna-Lynne, please visit her website at Jenna-Lynne.com

About the Publisher

Stolen Kiss Press is the publisher of the *Hurricane* series by Jenna-Lynne Duncan.

Stolen Kiss Press specializes in heart-stopping, page-turning, haunting romance in all genres.

For more information visit StolenKissPress.weebly.com